Sharyn crouched down in the freshly turned red clay. "So what's going on here?"

Glad to be back on a familiar subject, even if it involved a dead body, Nick dropped to the ground and took out his flashlight. "There's a guy buried in this car."

Sharyn sighed, regretting the abuse she was about to put her new uniform through. "Are we sure this person wasn't *meant* to be buried here in this car? This *is* a cemetery."

"I don't think he was meant to be buried a*live,* do you?"

"What?" She stretched out on the ground beside him.

Shining the flashlight through the partially buried car window, they could clearly see the outline of a body on the driver's side. It was half out of the car, like the man was trying to climb through the open window. The top half of his body was buried in the dirt.

Nick used the flashlight to illuminate the gloomy interior of the car. "I think he was alone. It looks like he was trying to get out."

D0556608

Last Rites

JOYCE & JIM LAVENE

W⊙RLDWIDE®

TORONTO • NEW YORK • LONDON
AMSTERDAM • PARIS • SYDNEY • HAMBURG
STOCKHOLM • ATHENS • TOKYO • MILAN
MADRID • WARSAW • BUDAPEST • AUCKLAND

Recycling programs
for this product may
not exist in your area.

LAST RITES

A Worldwide Mystery/November 2013

First published by Avalon Books.

ISBN-13: 978-0-373-26872-6

Copyright © 2004 by Joyce and Jim Lavene.

Printed in U.S.A.

For Lilla Juanita Messenger Pluth—1929–2003
I couldn't have done it without you, Mom!

~JEL

PROLOGUE

"How much longer do we have to do this?" Stevie half-heartedly pulled at some tall weeds in front of him.

"Until Mr. Willis says we've done enough to earn our civic duty badge," his friend informed him.

"But we've been out here all day. I wanted to try out the new Xbox before Paul gets home."

"Yeah. Your brother can be a real pain in the butt. I'm glad I have a sister. She only wants to play with Barbie."

The warm May sun beat down on their heads as they continued pulling weeds. There was no shade. Only one old pine tree stood at the edge of the pre–Civil War cemetery where they worked. It was gnarled and twisted, resembling a grotesque hand that seemed to be thrusting out of the ground. People in Diamond Springs used it as a marker for the city limit.

No one recalled the people who were buried there. Most of the tombstones had fallen over or rotted. Still, the Diamond Springs' Historical Society put a wreath on the rickety front gate every year. This year, Angelica Parsons, president of the Historical Society, had persuaded Tad Willis to take BSA Troop #323 to the cemetery and begin the cleanup.

"What's that?" Stevie asked his friend.

"What?"

"That thing over there. Something shiny. See it?"

"It looks like glass."

Stevie dropped to his knees and pushed at the weeds. "It's a car window! There's a car buried over here. Cool!"

His friend leaned closer and peered into the gloom. "What's that inside?"

"It looks like a man!"

Both boys ran to find the scoutmaster.

ONE

SHERIFF SHARYN HOWARD was up to her elbows in crushed tomatoes when the call came. Her copper-red hair was covered with flour. A pasta maker lay abandoned on her new kitchen table. Open boxes of ziti were on the cabinet beside her.

"Not now." She ignored the phone as she stirred the pasta into the boiling water. She read the directions on the box again.

She was determined to make dinner for Nick Thomopolis. He'd teased her mercilessly since she got her own apartment. He'd made dinner for her many times. The most she ever cooked for him was popcorn and pizza rolls. But all of that was about to change. She was finally living in her own place. It was small but she loved it. Even her mother had gotten over the fact that she didn't live at home anymore. The possibilities were endless.

She and Nick, the county medical examiner, had been seeing each other for about a year. They'd worked together for several years. She hadn't expected their working relationship to last after they got off to a rocky start. She *definitely* never thought they'd still be dating.

Dating? That can't be what you call it. There has to

be something more mature. She was thirty years old. Too old to *date.*

The phone rang again. This time it triggered her cell phone. They both clamored insistently for her attention. She stirred her homemade marinara sauce and checked her pasta. Everything was going smoothly. It was four-thirty. Nick would be there at six. She glanced around the messy kitchen. Clean up, a shower, and getting dressed would take about an hour. She buttered the fresh bread and cut open a clove of garlic.

There was a knock at the door as she began to clear the table. She looked up at the new café clock on the kitchen wall. Nick was never early. He *couldn't* be early now. She brushed some of the flour from her hair, wiped her hands on her tomato-smeared apron, and went to answer the door.

Head deputy Ernie Watkins was waiting for her. His gaze raced quickly from her bare feet to her flour-powdered hair. "What are you doing? Why aren't you dressed?"

"What are you talking about? Why are *you* here?" She silently dared him to say the words. This couldn't be happening. Not tonight. She'd planned everything so carefully. Couldn't whatever it was have waited until tomorrow?

"Both of your phones are ringing. I've left ten messages. Why do you *think* I'm here?"

She tried to ignore his less than charitable humor. It was only a few months since he called off his wedding to his childhood sweetheart. Since then, he was a lot like working with a bear. A short, wiry bear in a bad mood that made the single sprig of hair on the top of his head stand straight up. "This is the only day I've had off in six weeks. I don't care what happened or who it happened to. I'm going to clean up my kitchen, take a shower and put on my new sundress. Then I'm going to wait until Nick gets here with a nice bottle of wine and flowers. We're going to do what normal couples do for a change."

"You might be waiting a long time. Nick is already out at the cemetery. I don't know about the nice wine or the flowers. But he has some lovely sample bags, and a van with two lovesick assistants. I think that'll have to do you for tonight."

Sharyn fumed. "How am I ever supposed to make dinner for him when *you* keep finding dead people?"

"I guess making people unhappy is my special gift right now."

"Okay." She drew a deep breath and took pity on him. "What's happened *now?*"

THE TOW TRUCK was already backing up to the side of the cemetery when Sharyn and Ernie pulled up. The big black tires spun in the fresh, deep mud created by the frequent spring rains.

Ernie got out of the car and put on his hat. "What's Nick doing?"

Sharyn watched the Montgomery Country Medical Examiner jumping up and down and flailing his arms wildly in the air. "I don't know. He looks like he's having a fit of some kind."

Nick caught sight of them and rushed over to their car. Raindrops beaded on his black hair. His olive-skinned face was anxious. "You've got to stop them! If they pull that car out, it'll destroy the crime scene."

"You mean you didn't ask him to do it?" Sharyn looked at the tow-truck door. *Jamieson's Wrecker Service.* "Somebody called him. Rick doesn't come out for free."

"He's here at the request of our new police chief," Nick told her. "Do something!"

Ernie pushed his hat back on his head. "I'll do something."

Sharyn watched him run over to the driver who was trying to find a place to connect the big tow hook on the car. "When was Roy here?"

"Before *you!*" Nick's tone was irritated. "Where were you? I've been calling you for half an hour."

"I was making dinner for the special man in my life. He complains all the time about me only making popcorn." She put on the flat brown sheriff's hat and adjusted the gun in her holster before she put on her poncho. It was starting to rain. Just what she needed to make everything worse. "But I suppose you forgot all about that with the exciting chance to look at another dead body."

He watched her walk away, cursed himself in Greek, and stormed after her. "I didn't forget. I've got the wine and flowers in my SUV to prove it. And seeing another dead body is just another job for me. But it is my *job.*"

"You don't have to prove anything to me."

"Sharyn..."

Rick Jamieson loomed up out of the mist in front of her. "I got orders from the police chief to move this here vehicle."

She faced him down, not in the mood to argue with him. "Chief Tarnower doesn't have jurisdiction here in the county, Mr. Jamieson. I do. And I'm telling you that I'll have to arrest you for disturbing a crime scene if you do anything else besides getting your truck out of the field."

"Okay," he relented, "but I better get to move the car when you're ready, *and* I'm charging a service call for coming out here this time."

Ernie edged him away from Sharyn and back towards his truck. "That's fine, Rick. Just make sure to send that bill to the Diamond Springs *Police* Department and not to the sheriff."

Jamieson continued to gripe as he got in his truck, "When did everything get so complicated, Ernie? Why do we need two police departments anyway? It's just a waste of my tax money."

"You'll have to take that up with the county commission, my friend. I'll be sure to have Dr. Thomopolis give you a call when the car's ready to tow."

"That's the question lots of people are asking," Nick told Sharyn, hoping to end their brief spat.

"Maybe. But I just do what they tell me." She crouched down in the freshly turned red clay. "So what's going on here?"

Glad to be back on a familiar subject, even if it involved a dead body, Nick dropped to the ground and took out his flashlight. "There's a guy buried in this car."

Sharyn sighed, regretting the abuse she was about to put her new uniform through. Between not eating her mother's home cooking and regular workouts, she'd lost a size in her waist and hips. Her new uniforms didn't look any better than the old brown and tan ones. But they were smaller. And *that* was an accomplishment for a woman who couldn't smell chocolate without it adding ten pounds. "Are we sure this person wasn't *meant* to be buried here in this car? This *is* a cemetery."

"I don't think he was meant to be buried *alive*, do you?"

"What?" She stretched out on the ground beside him.

Shining the flashlight through the partially buried car window, they could clearly see the outline of a body on the driver's side. It was half out of the car, like the man was trying to climb through the open window. The top half of his body was buried in the dirt.

Nick used the flashlight to illuminate the gloomy interior of the car. "I think he was alone. It looks like he was trying to get out."

"Well, isn't *this* cozy?" Ernie stood over them. "What are we looking at?"

Sharyn got to her feet and brushed mud from her uniform. "Probably a murder."

"No wonder Roy wanted it so bad." He took her place on the ground and used his flashlight to look through the car window. "He hasn't had a murder investigation yet. That would be a feather in his new blue cap."

"You mean in his whole month as police chief?" Nick pulled out his cell phone. "Where are those kids? I swear, since I started paying them a salary they're even less reliable."

"I suppose it *would* be hard to decide if this old cemetery is in the town limits." Sharyn watched as one of the new, blue Diamond Springs police cars pulled up. Two brown sheriff's cars came in right behind it. "Do *we* know who gets this case?"

"Not yet." Ernie laughed. "Nine-one-one doesn't know who to give the emergency calls to either, I guess. But if it comes down to it, we have them outnumbered."

Chief Tarnower, looking like an enraged bulldog, stalked across the cemetery. Just behind him was his new sergeant, former sheriff's deputy David Matthews. "What's going on here, Sheriff? This cemetery is in *my* jurisdiction."

Sharyn refused to be drawn into the continuing argument. "Nice to see you, too, Roy. How's Matilda doing?"

"Don't think you can sweet talk your way around me like you do everybody else!" His face turned even redder as he wiped rain from his forehead. "Are you or are you not messing with my investigation?"

Nick stepped between them. "Jurisdiction? The M.E.'s office has jurisdiction over every crime scene. I know you're new to the game, Roy, but nothing moves until I say it moves. When you find a crime scene, you call me. Then I decide what gets done next."

Tarnower stood glaring at the taller man, his squat body shaking with rage. The rain came down harder as night began to settle around them. Mist rose from the old cemetery grounds like pitiful wraiths clinging to life. "I'm not *that* new to the game, son. And you're right. I should've checked with you before I started to move the car. It won't happen again."

"Thanks." Nick was surprised by his gruff admission. "I'm glad to hear that."

Roy faced Sharyn. "But that don't change things between you and me, missy. You and me got a reckoning coming."

She took a step around Nick and looked into the other man's face. "Walk with me, Roy."

Ernie shivered as rain slid down his back, despite the protection of his bright orange poncho. "I wouldn't want to be him. She wasn't in a good mood to begin with."

Nick folded his arms across his chest. "She was pretty ticked about dinner, huh?"

"Like a woman with a bee's nest in her bustle, son."

"I wouldn't want to be him, either. There are the kids and the van. Think you could get me some spotlights out here?"

"If it's *our* investigation."

"Excuse me?"

"Just funnin' you, Nick. I'll call the office and find you some spotlights. Don't start yelling at me, too. I get enough of that from the sheriff."

SHARYN AND ROY walked towards the drainage ditch that separated the cemetery from the gravel road. The area buzzed with deputies and officers trying to find something the other group couldn't find. Creating a local police department for the town of Diamond Springs had caused several jurisdictional incidents between the two groups. Each encounter got worse. It was like armed camps, each trying to outdo the other. They refused to find any common ground.

"We can't go on like this," Sharyn began. "There has to be a way we can work together."

"Okay. When are you gonna hand in your resignation? That's when we can work together."

She understood his anger and frustration but she didn't like it. Her hat's broad visor provided her some shelter from the rain as she stared at him. "Is that the way it has to be?"

He took off his narrow-banded cap and wiped his hand across his face. "I don't see any possibility of us ever working together. You're T Raymond's daughter. I never liked your daddy much when he was sheriff and I don't like you. Women don't have any place in law enforcement as far as I'm concerned." Roy grinned and hitched his wet belt up a little higher on his broad waist.

"If that's the way it is, I guess that's all there is to say. Except for one thing." Her voice took on the tone of command that she'd learned in the last few years as sheriff. "Don't ever show me a lack of respect in front of my deputies again. I'll treat you with the respect and courtesy your office demands and you'll treat me the same. We both uphold the law. You don't have to like me. But you *do* have to work with me."

She left him standing at the side of the ditch, holding his hat. Cases like this one were tricky. It was fine for the county commission to create a new law-enforcement division. The sheriff's department had their hands full. But who was going to decide which group worked on what case? She didn't see Julia Richmond or any of the other commissioners out there with Platt maps telling them if this cemetery was in the county, or still in the town limits of Diamond Springs.

Nick and his team were already working the area around the car. Ernie waited with his deputies, Joe Landers and Ed Robinson.

Even though it was almost dark, Joe didn't remove his sunglasses. His spiky brown hair didn't flatten out under the onslaught of rain. It wouldn't dare. "Is there really a dead guy in a car over there?"

"I'm afraid so," Sharyn answered, then spoke to Ernie. "Until we know whose jurisdiction this is we'll proceed like it's ours. Let's talk to those kids over there so they can go home."

Joe punched one leather-gloved fist into the palm of his other hand. "And you want me to take care of old Roy, right?"

"Not tonight." She laughed. "Go over and start taking notes on whatever Nick says. Let's try to stay one jump ahead on this. Ed, make sure we don't start building up traffic on the road."

Ed's hooded poncho was like Ernie's: Sheriff's Dept. emblazoned in fluorescent letters on the back. "What kind of car is that? You know, I've been having trouble with mine and I'm looking for a bargain. Think the county might auction it?"

"Maybe. Joe can tell you what kind of car it is later." Sharyn pulled up the hood on her poncho against the steady downpour. "But I don't think Trudy will be impressed by *any* car that we dig out of this cemetery."

"She doesn't have to know," Ed said.

"Get out in the street," Ernie instructed. "It's starting to look like a parking lot out there."

Sharyn and Ernie walked towards the old pine tree where the Boy Scouts were waiting. The cemetery ground was soft, making sucking sounds under their feet. The sweet smell of spring rain mingled with the scent of new honeysuckle and the good farmland that surrounded them.

Keeping his voice low, Ernie said, "I've already got Cari checking on the area. We should know pretty soon whose case this is."

"Thanks. How do you always manage to know what I need you to do?"

"Years of experience and a touch of the sight." He didn't try to act like he wasn't pleased by her words. "I guess we'll have to start carrying one of those GPS gizmos with us when we go out on cases."

"Only if you can get the County to cough up the money for them."

Tad Willis and his wife, Judy, were with the group of scouts. All of them were ready for the adventure to end.

"Sheriff, these kids are tired and cold. Their parents expected them home an hour ago. Can we leave now?"

Willis's glasses were fogged up. The glare from the flashlights made him look even more pale than usual.

Sharyn took him aside, leaving Ernie to speak to the scouts and Judy. "If you could talk me through what happened here and how you found the car, I don't see any reason for you to stay."

Willis, a local gallery owner from Diamond Springs, told her exactly how the two boys came to find the car and what they did afterwards. "I called nine-one-one right away. Then I brought all of the boys over here. I didn't want them gawking at it. What's it doing out here anyway? Is it some practical joke?"

She skirted his questions. "We don't know yet. Was there anyone else out here in the cemetery when you got here?"

"I didn't see anyone. And from the state this old place is in, I'd say no one's been here for a while. That's about all I can tell you."

"I appreciate your help, Mr. Willis. And I'm glad things have worked out all right for you and your family."

He glanced at his rain-soaked wife and sons. "Believe me, Sheriff. There won't ever be another Darva Richmond in my life."

She was glad to hear it. The woman had almost ruined him. "If I have any other questions for you, I'll give you a call. I'd appreciate a list of all the boys that are here tonight."

"Of course. No problem." He wiped his glasses on

his wet jacket and squinted at her. "You don't think *I* had anything to do with this, do you?"

"I'm sure everything will work out just fine. Go home, Mr. Willis. I'd hate for any of you to catch a cold out here." She escorted him back to the group without answering his question. It was too soon for her to know what was going on."

Ernie thanked the boys for their help and caught up with her a few yards away. "Not much there. They were pulling up some weeds and saw the car window. Judy didn't see anything."

"I didn't think so. This cemetery hasn't been touched in years. The chances are that the car has been here for a while."

Roy sauntered past them to conduct his own inter-rogation of the scouts and the scoutmaster. His good right-arm man nodded to the sheriff as he walked by.

"Sharyn."

"David."

Ernie glanced back at the former deputy. "I can't believe that boy took a job with Roy after everything we've done for him. He should've been out on the street a dozen times but you kept taking him back. Then Roy comes along with his shiny new police badge and David falls for it."

"It's not surprising. You know he always thought he should be sheriff. He's got a lot better chance of being police chief."

Nick stood next to the dark mound where the old car was still half-buried. Keith and Megan, his recently hired college student assistants, were busy trying to get pictures of the scene.

Ernie watched them for a minute. "Wouldn't it be easier to wait until someone brings the lights?"

"They need to have *something* to do," Nick said.

Sharyn watched as one of the new police officers got his uniform covered in red clay following the two assistant M.E.s around the scene. In contrast, Joe stood back, watching the parade. Years of experience had taught him that any real information would come from Nick. "Do we know anything yet?"

"Is that like, 'Are we having fun yet'?" Nick smiled at her.

"That's not going to help."

He took a step closer to her. "How about the roses? They're still fresh. I can go and get them."

She took a step away. "You were doing your job. I'm not holding it against you."

Ernie whistled through his teeth and shook his head.

Joe groaned and looked away. "That's trouble."

"Do you two mind?" Nick took another step closer to Sharyn. "We're trying to have an intimate moment."

"In a graveyard?" Ernie laughed.

"With a dead body sitting not ten feet away from you?" Joe applauded him. "I've been married for twenty years and even I wouldn't try *that*."

Nick wiped the rain from his face. "You can see how desperate I am. Besides, do you think it ever gets any better than this for us?"

They could hear Megan and Keith laughing even though they couldn't see them.

"Okay. That's enough." Sharyn shone her flashlight in Nick's face. "We can talk about this later. Could we get back to the case?"

Ernie looked at Joe. "That was cold, wasn't it?"

Joe ignored the rain that slid down his sunglasses. "Arctic."

Headlight beams shone into the cemetery as another car joined the group. Sheriff's Deputy Marvella Honeycutt's raspy baritone cut through the rain and the mist. "Where do you want these lights?"

"Over here!" Nick put his arm around Sharyn's shoulders and planted a quick kiss on her mouth. "Gotta go. Some of us have work to do. When I know something about what we're looking at, I'll call."

Ernie clapped him on the shoulder. "Nice move."

"Yeah," Joe agreed. "Now you'd better get away fast."

Sharyn was used to being teased about her relationship with Nick. Being sheriff made her a public figure. Nothing she did was hidden for long. It was one of the reasons she'd taken so long deciding to let him into her life. But despite everything, she was glad he was there. "I'm going home. Stay here, Joe, and keep an eye on things. Ernie, if you're done laughing, you can drive me home."

Marvella came trudging through the mud with a large flood lamp across her shoulders. "Sounds to me like you're having a party out here. Cari told me to bring these lights out. But I think someone else can get the generator out of the trunk. That sucker's heavy!"

"Thanks." Even in the dim lights, Sharyn could see that her newest deputy was wearing a hot-pink poncho. It definitely wasn't issued by the sheriff's department. But she wasn't going to tackle her continued fashion statements tonight.

"What's going on out here anyway?" Marvella asked, taking in the scene.

"Dead guy in a car." Ernie walked past her. "We're leaving. Help them get those lights set up and you can leave, too."

Marvella's face was invisible in the depths of her hood, but her voice was as strident as ever. "Well thank you, Mr. Grumpy Pants. I know you're having a bad time right now, which you wouldn't be having if you'd listened to me. But you don't have to take it out on the rest of us."

He didn't answer. The door to the squad car slammed shut behind him.

Sharyn got in the car beside him. "Did she really call you Mr. Grumpy Pants?"

The gravel spun under the tires as he pulled out. "I told you it was a mistake to make that woman a deputy."

"She does a good job, Ernie."

"Maybe so. But she's almost irritated me to death. Doesn't that count for something?"

They drove back to her apartment. It was unusually quiet between them. She knew he was depressed about his breakup with Annie. She'd tried to get him to talk about it but he wasn't interested. She'd known him all of her life. He was the one who kept her going when she first became sheriff. He was her father's best friend. "Would you like to come up for a cup of coffee?"

"Nah. I'd better get back to the motel. They might lock me out if I come in too late."

"Yeah. I hear the Motel Six can be pretty strict." She paused and tried to find the right words. "Ernie—"

"Please don't ask me if I need a place to stay again. I'm fine where I am."

"No, you're not. It's too bad you sold your house, and things didn't work out with Annie. But you can't keep punishing yourself forever. What happened between you and Cari was—"

"Stupid? Insane?"

"Both," she admitted. "But everybody does stupid, insane things from time to time. How many times have you told me that?"

His face was bleak in the dim light from the dash. "I'll be fine, Sharyn. Go on inside and clean up your mess."

"All right. But I'm here if you need me. And so is my apartment."

His voice was husky. "Thanks. I'll see you tomorrow."

THE KITCHEN WAS finally clean. Sharyn managed to scrub the tomato sauce from under her nails and the flour out of her hair. Cooking wasn't as easy or as neat as her mother made it look. It might take years and a fortune in cookbooks to figure it out.

She'd just settled down with a torrid romance novel when the phone rang. Thinking it was probably Nick with some information about the car in the cemetery, she picked it up without looking away from the book.

"Sheriff Howard?" The voice was nasal with a heavy, backwoods Southern accent.

"Yes. Who's this?"

"Skeeter Johnson."

She dropped her book. A flash of pain stabbed at her chest. She sat forward to take a deep breath. It was all she could do to speak. "What can I do for you, Mr. Johnson?"

"I know you hate me. And you got good reason. And you got no good reason to believe what I'm gonna tell you. But it's the honest truth. May heaven strike me dead if it's not."

She was holding the phone so tightly that her knuckles were white. With an effort, she forced herself to relax. He couldn't hurt her anymore. "What do you want?"

"I want to atone. I want to be forgiven."

"Not by *me*."

He laughed a little. "No, not by you. I don't need your forgiveness, Sheriff. But I need your help to make it right."

She wanted to throw the phone across the room. She didn't want to listen to anything he had to say. But she forced herself to stay on the line.

"Maurice and me weren't the only ones involved in shooting your daddy. We only did it for the money."

JOYCE & JIM LAVENE 27

She closed her eyes and tried not to see her father's dead body on the convenience store floor again. "You mean the sixty-seven dollars you got from the cash register? I don't think that was worth his life."

Skeeter cleared his throat. "I mean the two thousand that somebody *paid* us to kill him. Somebody important. Somebody who should be right here with me and Maurice in prison."

"Who?" She could barely breathe. After years of suspecting her father's death was something more than a random murder, she might finally be able to prove it. "Who was it?"

TWO

"I WANT TO ATONE, Sheriff. But I ain't stupid. You come up here. Bring a lawyer with you. I don't expect nothin' out of it. I'm just not ready to die yet."

Sharyn gritted her teeth. "I'll be up there tomorrow. But you'd better have something important for me."

"I'll be waiting, Sheriff. There's some bad stuff goin' down right there in Diamond Springs. People think it's all pretty houses and roses. But I know better. See you tomorrow."

The line went dead but she didn't move for a long time. Finally, she put down the phone and sat on the sofa.

Sheriff Sharyn Howard was the third generation of law enforcement in her family. Her grandfather, Jacob Howard, was the first man elected as sheriff of Diamond Springs, North Carolina. Her father, T Raymond Howard, had been sheriff of Montgomery County for almost twenty years. He was killed while he bought some milk one Sunday morning.

Sharyn had just finished law school when it happened. Ernie, who was her father's head deputy, too, came to tell her about it. She insisted on going back to the store with him. Despite the fact that she was raised in and around the sheriff's department, she couldn't believe that that was her father lying in a pool of his own blood. She knew she'd never forget that moment. It was etched in her mind, even though he'd been dead for five years.

The county commission had called for a special election to replace T Raymond, since it was in the middle of his term. Her father's political party had asked her to run for sheriff. They figured she'd get the sympathy vote and they could always find a serious candidate later. She agreed and won the election against Deputy Roy Tarnower. Her first case was to solve her father's murder.

On a cold, wet February day, Sharyn and her deputies cornered the two men who killed her father. Skeeter ran out the back of the old barn. Ernie, Ed and Joe were in the front. Without thinking or calling for backup, she pursued him. She took out her grandfather's WWII service revolver that she'd chosen to carry and shot him when he refused to stop. Skeeter went down in the old cornfield but not before he returned fire, hitting her in the leg.

Skeeter was only wounded in the shoulder. He got up and kept running. Sharyn lay on the ground, unable to follow him. She tried to make a tourniquet but couldn't stop the bleeding. She'd lost her radio and couldn't tell her deputies what had happened.

But Ernie was right behind her. He called for the paramedics as he ran by her. Ed and Joe had already taken Maurice Semple, Skeeter's partner, to the squad car in handcuffs. They stayed with her until the ambulance got there. By that time, Ernie was leading Skeeter back to the barn.

Afterwards, Ernie threatened her with all manner of terrible things if she did anything like that again. She knew what she did was wrong and might have cost her her life. She'd never done anything that stupid again.

In record time, the jury convicted both men of killing her father. They were sentenced to life in prison. If T Raymond had been in uniform that morning, they would've been given the death penalty. Sharyn had been satisfied with the verdict anyway. She grew into the job and became the "serious candidate" her backers were looking for. And last year, she'd won another election against Roy Tarnower.

But never once at the trial did Semple or Johnson say anything about someone paying them to kill her father. She didn't know if she believed it. But she couldn't ignore it.

Sharyn went to the kitchen and opened the refrigerator door. She closed it again without touching any food. The answer to her frustration wasn't in eating. All of her life, she'd had a weight problem. She was finally getting it under control. She couldn't let those terrible memories put her back on that merry-go-round. There wasn't anything she could eat to keep that gnawing ache from her soul.

Instead, she put on some jeans and a black sweater. She tucked her grandfather's revolved into the holster that rested against her back and looked in the bathroom mirror. She was always the sheriff. No matter what she did or where she went. She wished she'd realized the burden her father carried while he was alive. It wasn't easy. She wanted to tell him that she understood, and have him smile at her again. But that wasn't going to happen.

Her shoulder-length copper curls were still damp. Impatiently, she ran a comb through them and put the whole mass up in a ponytail. Her square-chinned, freckled face and blue eyes stared back at her. She looked like her father and all the other Howards. Maybe that was why she'd agreed to continue carrying the burden of being sheriff. It was in her blood.

She switched off the lights in her apartment, pulled on a black-hooded windbreaker, and walked out the door. Diamond Springs was asleep around her as she prowled the streets. The Uwharrie Mountains were black sentinels shadowing the small town.

Diamond Mountain Lake glittered in the heart of the downtown area. New growth was bringing expensive houses and condos to the lakeshore, and money into the pockets of the county commission. But the old red-brick high school where Sharyn graduated was still the same. Its sloping roof and old oaks reminded her of the way things were when she was growing up there. Unfortunately, like everything else, good things changed, too.

She turned away from the wet wind that blew off the lake. The scent of water and pine trees followed her past the shuttered windows of the century-old Regency Hotel. Across the street, the theater slept, the front face plastered with posters for a new performance of *Macbeth*. It made the old structure look like a silent movie queen with bad makeup.

Sharyn loved Diamond Springs. It was as much a part of her family as her parents and her sister. She knew the mountains and the streets as intimately as she knew her own face. Her ancestors rested beneath the great oaks at the Presbyterian Church just outside town. On nights like this, she couldn't help but think about herself being there with them one day. Her spirit would roam the streets, like people said that Cara Sommers's ghost haunted the schoolyard where she was killed.

As usual when she couldn't sleep, she wound up at the sheriff's office. The little structure next to the pink granite courthouse was more her home than any place else. But that was changing, too. The boxes and crates that met her when she switched on the light reminded her that nothing ever stayed the same. The county commission decided that it would be better to house the newly created police department here.

They allocated money for a new sheriff's department to be built at the site of the Clement's Building. The old Capitol Insurance office was destroyed by fire when Sharyn was still in high school. It was only recently razed after a final arson investigation that had rocked Diamond Springs last year. The county was building a bigger, more modern sheriff's office. There would be a larger holding area for prisoners who were on their way to the county lockup. It was good. It was progress.

But this place that was built for her grandfather, and

held so many memories of her father and her childhood, would always be special. She walked through each of the empty offices and the conference room. The county was refurbishing the building. Most of the walls were already stripped and in the process of being repainted. The sagging wood floors were being replaced, as well.

The only room untouched was her office. With a sigh, she began packing up the rest of her possessions. Almost everything had already been moved to the temporary sheriff's office located in the basement of the courthouse. Her father's big desk was going into storage until the new building was finished. There wasn't room for it in the cramped, temporary quarters.

She taped and marked a few boxes of personal items then rolled up the big wall map of Montgomery County. Leaning against the side of the desk, she looked at the two portraits on the old green wall. Her grandfather scowled back at her. Even her father's blue eyes seemed to be unforgiving.

"It's not like I had any choice in the matter." Her voice echoed in the hollow room. "I suppose you could've found a way to stop it?" She shook her head at her flights of fancy. A sheriff probably shouldn't have an imagination that led to talking to pictures in the middle of the night.

She felt as though she'd let Jacob and T Raymond down. Maybe she should've fought harder to stay at this site. Maybe she should've exerted some pressure on the commission not to create a separate city police force.

But she tried to use her influence wisely. She already understood how it could be misused.

She'd learned so much since she'd become sheriff. Most of it wasn't pleasant. Including the innuendos about how her father and several of the powerful men in the community ran things. She didn't have proof that any of it was true. And sometimes she wished she wasn't like a bear with a thorn in its paw about looking for the truth.

She realized tomorrow could change all of that. When she talked to Skeeter, she might finally be able to piece some things together. She hoped that she could live with it when she did.

Reining in her imagination, she went to the wall and took down her grandfather's portrait. Jacob Howard's stern visage was only apparent when he was in uniform. Her memories of him included watching him laugh in the sunshine as he did his lucky-fishing dance. He was always patient with her, always ready to indulge her curiosity—like the time the ants escaped from their homemade ant farm, much to her mother's dislike.

Sharyn wrapped the portrait carefully and put it into a box. She wouldn't try to find a place for it until they made the final move into the new office. She took down her father's portrait, tracing his familiar face with her finger. There wasn't a day that she didn't miss him. Even now, she could still feel the sickening blow when Ernie told her that he was dead. It never occurred to her that he would die. Especially not like that.

She finally wrapped the portrait carefully in newspaper and set it on top of the other one. She looked back at the wall and gasped. There were two discolored outlines where the portraits had hung. They probably hadn't been moved in at least twenty years. But in the rectangular area where her father's portrait had been was a small wood panel. It was flush against the wall.

A thousand thoughts rushed through her head. Jack Winter, long time district attorney of Montgomery County, now a state senator, had been looking for something in her father's den at their home last year. When he couldn't find it, he had the house set on fire so that no one else would find it, either.

She couldn't prove that he was responsible for the break-in at her mother's house or the fire, but she *knew* there was something going on between him and her father. Jack was capable of having her father killed. She had no doubt about that. But if T Raymond was one of his cohorts in crime, what happened that caused Jack to turn on him? She'd thought for a while that her father might have some evidence against Jack that he planned to use.

She tried to open the panel in the wall but it had been closed for a long time. She had to use her letter opener to pry it open. No paint came away with it, which meant it was installed after the last paint job at the sheriff's office. She wasn't sure when that happened. It seemed to her that the walls had always been that terrible shade of green.

Behind the panel, a small area had been hollowed out between the two-by-four wall braces. It was rough, no backing except the old wall board behind it. On either side, pink insulation showed through. The only thing inside was a small, black book. It looked like the kind of thing an accountant would use. She wiped the dust off it with her sleeve and opened it.

Numbers and letters in no certain order filled the pages. She knew the handwriting belonged to her father. He had an odd way of writing that he attributed to being left-handed. She'd teased him about it so often, there was no mistaking it. She flipped through all of the pages but none of them made any sense. There were letters at the top of each entry, like dates, but indecipherable. What could they mean? More important, was this what Jack was looking for at her mother's house?

Sharyn heard the back door to the sheriff's office open and close. Ernie called her name and started walking towards her office. Quickly, she hid the book in her jacket then closed the panel in the wall.

Ernie was T Raymond's best friend and deputy for more than twenty years. She'd grown up expecting to see him every day like she did her father. She trusted him with her life. But there were many times since her father died that she knew he'd held the truth back from her. She didn't want him to know what she'd found until she had a chance to really look at it.

He looked around as he walked into her office. "I saw the light on. I knew it had to be you. What's up?"

"Nothing. I just couldn't sleep. Thought I'd come and try to finish up this mess."

He started to sit down but she stopped him, rushing him out of the office as she switched off the light. "Let's go get something to eat. I don't know about you, but I'm starving."

"Sure. I could eat. You're kind of jumpy. Are you sure nothing's wrong?"

She pulled on her jacket, mindful of the book. "Just the usual. Skeeter Johnson called me from prison."

"What in blazes did *he* want?"

"He wants to atone before he dies. Apparently, he's found religion. He says he has information about Dad's death. He told me someone important paid him and Maurice to kill him."

They crossed deserted Main Street together. The green neon coffee shop light beckoned them to the only all-night diner in town.

"You don't believe that, do you?"

"I don't know yet. I'm going up there tomorrow. He wants me to bring a lawyer to document everything. I called Jill Madison-Farmer. I think it's worth a trip to Raleigh to hear what he has to say."

Ernie sat in a booth. "That boy couldn't tell the truth if his life depended on it."

"You don't think it's possible?" Sharyn ordered coffee from the waitress, then waited until she left to add, "You don't think the good-old-boy network might have had Dad killed?"

He glanced around the nearly empty diner then leaned close to her. "Why would they?"

"Are you asking that because he always did everything Jack Winter and Caison Talbot wanted?"

"No!" Ernie sat back and nervously fingered his mustache. "T Raymond wasn't like that. You know better. But he could never prove anything that was done, either. There was no reason to kill him."

"Jack was after something in Dad's den, Ernie. Maybe Dad had something that he didn't tell you about. Maybe it got him killed."

The waitress brought their coffee and they ordered breakfast. It was barely 3:00 a.m. but there were a few other people who had wandered into the diner, too.

"You're gonna get yourself killed, Sharyn." Ernie's voice was purposely low. "You can't go after these people without something happening. You've already seen that!"

"Weren't you just telling me that there's nothing to the idea that they killed Dad? Why would they kill me?"

Before he could answer, Deputy Cari Long joined them. With David gone, Cari was the youngest sheriff's deputy. Her long blond hair was tied back from her pretty face. She was out of uniform in a light blue sweater and jeans. She smiled at Ernie, her brown eyes wistful. But she sat beside Sharyn.

Ernie sipped his coffee but didn't look at her. It had been that way between them since a late-night kiss— exchanged while they were working together—ended his engagement.

"I got the information about the cemetery that you wanted." Cari was talking to him but looking at Sharyn. "It's right on the edge, but it's out of town so it's ours."

Sharyn had watched them over the last few months

since the incident. It wasn't getting any better. They spent too much time avoiding each other, sending messages to each other through other people. She'd tried to be sensitive to the issue but she wouldn't let their personal issues upset their work anymore. "I'm really tired all of a sudden. I think I'm going home."

Cari looked up at her with something like terror in her eyes. "But your breakfast just got here!"

"Maybe you can eat it and keep Ernie company while you tell him what he asked you to find out. I'll see you both later at the office."

Ernie got to his feet. "I could walk you back."

Sharyn put one hand on his shoulder and the other on Cari's. "The two of you need to move on. What's done is done. There's no way to go back. You'll just have to move forward. And that's about all the cliches that I can think of right now. Good night. Next time I see you, I want you to be talking to each other."

Ernie sat back down and picked up his coffee cup with a determined hand. "Yes, ma'am." He glanced at Cari. She peeped out at him.

Sharyn clutched the book she'd found in her office to her side under her jacket and walked out of the diner.

AT 7:45 THAT MORNING, Sharyn was waiting outside the gate at the North Carolina Corrections Facility in Raleigh. She'd left Diamond Springs three hours earlier. She didn't ask anyone to go with her. This was something she wanted to do alone.

A white Volvo wagon pulled up next to her red

Jeep. Jill Madison-Farmer took her briefcase out of the car and adjusted her black designer suit. Her tinted blond hair was highlighted by the sunlight that filtered through the clouds. When she saw Sharyn, she walked quickly to her side. "Good morning, Sheriff."

"Good morning. Thanks for coming on such short notice."

"No problem. Especially if what you told me turns out to be true. I've taken more than one strange case to move up the ladder. This one could put my name in the books."

The morning breeze was cold as they waited for the guard to open the front gate. Sharyn could see some of the prisoners walking the empty grounds. She didn't recognize any of them but she knew she'd put away a fair share since she'd taken office.

She wanted to see Jack Winter walking across the gravel yard, wearing prison garb. She made herself think rationally about it. Her job demanded proof and there was nothing she could prove he'd done. Nothing except the sure knowledge that he was always watching her. And while that was irritating, she could hardly cite it as cause for an arrest warrant. He was connected well enough to win an election to the senate. She needed something substantial against him.

The two women signed in at the gate. Both of them surrendered their weapons. They walked into the facility together. It had been a few years since Sharyn had been there but nothing much had changed. The building was still stark and gray. Its cheerless exterior only gave way as protection from the elements. Nothing inside showed any warmth or humanity.

"This place gives me the creeps." Jill shivered as they walked down the long corridor that led to the visitation area.

"Have you been here before?"

"Yes. I brought my kids up here to show them what it was like."

"That was pretty ruthless of you."

Jill's even, white teeth looked like a toothpaste ad. "Thanks. I try to be a good mother."

"Did it work?"

"So far. But they're only six and eight. I'll let you know." Jill opened up her compact when the guard led them into a small, dark room. She checked her hair and lipstick as she sat down. "Any real idea on what he plans to tell you?"

"I'm not sure," Sharyn answered. "I told you everything he said on the phone last night."

Robert "Skeeter" Johnson, looking well muscled and fed, shuffled into the room a few minutes later with a burly guard at each arm. His gold tooth was gone but his smile showed a full set of white teeth provided by the state. They gleamed against his black skin. "Good to see you, Sheriff."

"Skeeter," she acknowledged.

He sat down and waited until the guards left to smile at Jill. "You are one *fine* lady. Don't tell me you're a lawyer."

"Jill Madison-Farmer." She extended her manicured

hand to him. "I've been an attorney for five years. I'm here to represent your interests."

"My interests." He ruminated over the word for a few seconds.

"You said you had something you wanted to tell me." Sharyn jogged him out of his reverie. "Something about my father's death."

"I ain't forgot, Sheriff." He smiled at Jill again. "She's always impatient. Did she tell you she was so impatient to catch me that she shot me? I could show you my scar."

Sharyn got to her feet. "I don't have time for this."

Skeeter laughed. "No time to put the man who *really* killed your daddy behind bars? I think you should pray for some patience, Sheriff. Now, your daddy, he was always a patient man. He was a good man. And if me and Maurice didn't need that money so bad, we wouldn't'a killed him dead."

It was all Sharyn could do to stand there and grit her teeth. It was good that they made them leave their weapons outside. It was bad enough that she wanted to pound the information out of him just to wipe that silly smile off of his face. She still wanted to shoot him again and again, the way he and Maurice had shot her father.

"Okay. Okay." He laughed. "I asked you to come here. I won't tease you anymore. Sit down, Sheriff. Let me tell you what I know."

Sharyn sat back down on the uncomfortable wooden chair and stared at him.

He sobered when he looked into her eyes. "A man

called me and Maurice two days before we killed your daddy. He said he'd pay us two thousand dollars before the job and another two thousand dollars after it was done. We knew where you lived. We waited until we saw the sheriff leave that morning. We could see he wasn't wearing his gun. We followed him into the store and shot him. Then we ran."

"Did the man give you the money before you shot him?" Sharyn asked, trying to put her anger and grief behind her.

"He dropped it off on that same day he called. We didn't see him but he was riding in a big, black limousine. Nice car."

"Did you see the license plate?" Jill questioned. "Was there anything about the car that you might recognize?"

"Nope. We didn't care about nothing like that." He sat back in his chair. "We bought a car with that money. We drove back to the Bridge Motel to meet him for the second half. He never showed up."

"Why didn't you say any of this at the trial?" Sharyn demanded.

"Because I recognized his voice on the phone. I knew it wasn't healthy for me to say that the district attorney paid me to kill the sheriff."

Sharyn felt weak, light-headed. All this time, she'd come so close to guessing what happened. She'd looked for the connection for so long that finally hearing it was almost too much.

"Do you have any way to prove that?" Jill queried. "Just telling us that the voice *sounded* like Jack Winter on the phone isn't going to cut it. Especially since you waited so long to come forth with it."

Sharyn was glad that Jill was there to ask the important questions when her own mind felt like tapioca.

"I wouldn't waste your time if I didn't have proof, pretty mama." He smiled again. "But now's the part where you tell me what you can do to help old Skeeter. I gave you what I had in good faith. What have you got for *me?*"

Jill glanced through the papers in her briefcase. "We can probably get your sentence reduced if you agree to testify at Winter's trial. It all depends on your proof."

"I want a reduced sentence for me and Maurice," Skeeter told her. "And we want to do it in the county lockup. The food's decent there and the guards ain't so mean. You get me that and we got a deal."

"Tell us what the proof is," Sharyn finally contributed to the conversation. "We can't do anything until we know that."

He folded his arms across his chest. They were full of scars from knife fights and needle marks. "You get me the deal, I give you the proof. Call me. You know my number."

JILL'S HEELS TAPPED double time on the tile behind Sharyn's longer strides. "Slow down, Sheriff. I know you're angry but losing me in here won't help you out any."

Sharyn complied, wondering what had possessed the other woman to wear heels to the prison in the first place. "I'm not angry."

"Yeah. Right. And I'm a rock singer."

"You'll never be able to get that deal for them. We both know that. And even if we agreed to testify to what we just heard, a judge would throw us out of the courtroom." Sharyn held the door as they exited the prison structure. "There's nothing else we can do."

"I know we don't exactly see things from the same point of view but I have a few friends who owe me some favors," Jill offered. "They might be able to help us with this."

"I can't afford your billable hours. I'll have to do this my own way."

"I would think, as sheriff, that you'd understand the value of teamwork. I don't want to charge you for this. But if we find something, I'll take my share of the applause. You know how hard it is to get a lucrative practice going these days?"

Sharyn smiled at the older woman in her Liz Claiborne suit and Gucci shoes. "All right. There may not be anything substantial to this. He could be lying."

Jill agreed as they reached her car. "Then I've wasted my time. Let me check it out. I might surprise you. I'm not as useless as I look."

Laughing at her similar thoughts, Sharyn held out her hand to the other woman. "Thanks for your help. Let me know if you find anything."

"I will. You keep me posted, too. How's that thing going between your aunt and Sam Two Rivers? I thought they might get married when I got him off on that murder charge."

"Not yet. Aunt Selma has lived alone for a long time. I don't know if she's even thought about it. Have a safe journey back, Jill. I'll talk to you later."

"WELL LOOK, FOLKS! It's the sheriff of Montgomery County!" Ernie's voice reached Sharyn's ears before she could take her jacket off at the door.

"You've got a pile of messages." Her assistant, Trudy, Ed's new fling, handed her about twenty pieces of pink memo paper. "A few reporters were here this morning about the body in the cemetery. Your mother wants to have lunch with you. And Nick called at least a hundred times."

Sharyn put the messages on her desk. It was actually a card table set about five feet from Trudy's card table. The basement of the courthouse was small, besides being dark and damp, no matter how many lights they added. It made her regret all the times she'd teased Nick about his office in the basement morgue of the hospital.

"Where have you been?" Ernie was in her face. "Since when do you just take off without a word to anyone? If you went to Raleigh, you should've said something. You are the sheriff here, you know."

She put her hat on her desk and took off her gun. She missed the privacy the old office gave them. Right now, a dozen pairs of eyes were watching them and the same number of ears were waiting to hear what she had to say. "Thanks, Trudy. I'll get back with Nick and my mother."

Ernie continued his tirade. "I can't be everywhere.

You have to tell me what's going on if I'm going to do my job."

"Could we talk about this later? I need to return these calls."

His left eye twitched with irritation. "I suppose we can. Can you schedule me in?"

She didn't try to call him back as he stalked away from her. There was really no reason for it. What she did in Raleigh had nothing to do with anything they were working on at the moment. Besides, his desk was only a few feet away in the same room. He was going to hear about anything she did. She took a deep breath and picked up the phone.

THREE

"WE FOUND HIS wallet buried in the car with him. I guess whoever killed him wasn't worried about anyone finding out who he was. The chances were pretty good that no one would ever find the car out there." Nick's voice sounded strange on the phone. "Where were you this morning?"

Sharyn sat back in her chair. "How long has he been dead?"

"I'm not sure yet. At least a few years. Where were you?"

She sighed. Didn't someone warn her about having a relationship with a coworker? If not, they should have. "It's a long story. I'd like to know more about the man in the car. Are you *sure* this wasn't a special-request burial? Did you check it out?"

"Besides the fact that this isn't Paris, and he was trying to get *out* of the car when he died? As sure as I have plenty of time for you to tell me where you were all morning."

"It's not a big deal, Nick. I went up to the prison in Raleigh. Nothing happened."

"Were you expecting something to happen? Or was

this just a joy ride because you didn't have anything else to do?"

"It's personal and I don't want to talk about it right now. I'll tell you at dinner. My place. Six-thirty?"

He grunted irritably but agreed. "I'll be there. Are we having the leftover pasta?"

"You got it. See you then. Keep me posted." She hung up the phone, pushing thoughts about Skeeter and Jack out of her mind.

"I got this fax earlier." Trudy brought her the sheet of paper.

Sharyn looked around the basement. Ed and Joe were back from their morning patrol. Ernie was at his desk, scowling. Cari sat off by herself at another small table. "Well, we're all nice and cozy here together so we might as well talk about the dead man the Boy Scouts found in the car yesterday."

Ed groaned into his coffee cup. "Don't tell me—it's a murder!"

Joe slapped him on the back. "Duh! The man was buried alive in his car! Not many people die of natural causes that way."

"Never mind that fooling around," Ernie reprimanded them. "Go ahead, Sheriff."

Sharyn felt like she was back in school again. "Thank you, Deputy. As you probably know already, Cari discovered that the old Union Cemetery is within our jurisdiction. That makes this our investigation. Don't everybody applaud all at the same time."

Trudy put down her coffee cup. "Couldn't we just

tell Roy that it's in his jurisdiction after all? I mean, he *wants* to solve a murder case real bad. He might not even question it."

"Good idea. But it's too late for that." Sharyn held up the front page of the *Diamond Springs Gazette.* "They have Platt maps, too, I guess."

The lead story was about the buried car, complete with pictures and quotes from the Boy Scouts who found it. For once, the *Gazette* wasn't questioning the sheriff's department's ability to solve the case. In fact, they were saying that it was better for the more experienced group to handle it.

"I read that this morning," Joe said. "I almost choked on my sausage. Since when is Foster Odom on our side?"

Ed laughed. "And how scary is it for him to be on our side? I like it better when he's against us!"

"If we could get back to the investigation?" Sharyn put down the newspaper. "Nick thinks the body inside the car was a man named Clint Walker. There was a wallet in his back pocket. They're looking for medical records, et cetera, to positively ID him."

"Nice of whoever it was to bury him with his wallet," Cari quipped. "Makes our job *easier.*"

"Well, he *was* buried in that old cemetery. Nobody ever goes out there," Joe observed. "They probably didn't expect anyone to find him."

"Maybe," Sharyn admitted. "Nick isn't finished with the autopsy yet, but apparently the man has two bullets in him. He isn't sure how long the body has been there and Megan and Keith are still working on the car and the burial site. So our information is limited. But Nick faxed me a copy of Mr. Walker's driver's license and Social Security card. He's listed as living in Diamond Springs. So we'll get started tracking the ID down and see what we can find out about him."

"I know the man's dead," Ed complained. "But can't Nick tell from the picture on the license if it's the same man?"

"No." Sharyn cleared her throat. "Decomposition was pretty bad."

No one asked her to explain any further.

"I can do a lot of that ID research on the computer," Cari volunteered, taking them away from the images in their minds.

"That sounds good. Find out whatever you can from the information we have." Sharyn had Trudy pass Cari a copy of the fax. "Just because this license was on the body doesn't mean it's the right license. Since his death wasn't an accident, it could be something the killer did intentionally to throw us off track."

Joe looked at the fax. "This license was two years out of date when he was buried."

"Let's hope someone didn't kill him for that," Sharyn replied. "While Cari's doing that, you and Ed can check out the address associated with the Social Security card. It's probably where he lived as a kid. Find out if anyone there knows where he is. Ernie and I will check out the address on the license."

"This is so exciting," Trudy gushed. "I never get to sit in on these meetings. Maybe I should be a deputy, too!"

Trudy had been the sheriff's assistant since Sharyn's father was there. She ran the office with a precision that was almost perfect. The idea of her changing positions was overwhelmingly rejected by the group.

"You know, it's one thing to be in the office talking about it, darlin'," Ed rushed to assure her, "but it's a whole other thing being out in the field."

"Yeah." Joe polished his sunglasses while he squinted in the fluorescent light. "It's dirty. You'd get your hair mussed. You wouldn't like it."

Ed told him to stay out of it. He'd been going out with Trudy for a few months after a lengthy battle to prove himself to her. He knew how stubborn she was. "Don't pay him any attention. You could handle being a deputy. But why would you want to? Besides, I don't think the sheriff plans to replace David anytime soon."

Sharyn intercepted Ed's beseeching look. He'd changed a lot since he and Trudy got together. He'd stopped flirting with every waitress, and running around town with every woman who fell for his good looks and sweet talk. She really believed he was serious this time. "He's right. I'm sorry, Trudy. Even if you wanted to be a deputy, I couldn't hire you yet. We can't hire another deputy until we move into our new location."

Trudy tossed her brown curls. Her husband of thirty years had been killed in an accident at the racetrack a few years back. She'd survived, despite her four grown children worrying about her. She could take care of herself. "Then maybe I should see what the police department has to offer! Maybe *they* wouldn't think I was useless. Roy and I got along pretty well when he was a deputy."

Ernie couldn't believe it. "Trudy, you don't want to do *that!*"

She snatched up her pocketbook. "Maybe I do. Especially since none of you think I'm capable of doing exactly what Marvella did. I talked to her about it. *She* thinks I can do the job. I know as much or more about being a deputy than most of you here!"

"Marvella is nothing but trouble," Ernie mumbled to himself.

Ed put his arm around Trudy's shoulders. "Let's talk about it, huh? Nobody's saying you can't do anything. Joe and I will check out this address and then we'll have some lunch. We could go to that corn dog stand you like so much."

Trudy's pretty face was still defiant. But she scooted her pocketbook back under her makeshift desk and plopped down in her folding chair. "All right. *For now.*"

Ed kissed her forehead. "That's my girl."

"You know how much I appreciate you being here, don't you?" Sharyn asked Trudy as Ed and Joe started up the basement stairs. "Being here is hard on everybody. There's not enough room to turn around in. I didn't mind losing David. But I need *you.*"

"Thanks, Sheriff." Trudy put a call on hold. "It just makes me so mad that everyone acts like they know so much more than me! Maybe I could just sit in on your meetings from now on? It makes the work seem so much more important."

Sharyn didn't have a problem with that idea. "That's fine with me. We'll talk again when I get back."

Trudy frowned as she watched Ernie and Sharyn disappear up the stairs. "And everybody goes out to check what's going on while I stay here and answer the phone like always. The story of my life."

"You could help me look up information on the computer, if you like," Cari offered.

"No, that's all right." Trudy picked up the phone that was ringing. "Sheriff's office."

"WELL, THAT BEATS ALL!" Ernie couldn't let it rest. "I've known Trudy for over twenty-five years and I've never heard her say anything so crazy."

Employees of the sheriff's department had to walk down through the new courthouse annex to reach their cars. Parking spaces at the courthouse were at a premium. Sharyn waved to Charlie, a retired sheriff's deputy, who was feeding the guard dogs that were kept to protect the parking and impound lot in the back of the old sheriff's office. "It's not crazy. She just wants to see what else she can do."

Ernie stared at her as they pulled out on Main Street, past the ornate antebellum homes that stood behind the hundred-year-old oaks across from the courthouse. "Are you saying she should be a deputy, too?"

"I don't think she really wants to be a deputy. I'm

saying that she's gone through a lot of changes in the past few years. The only thing that's stayed the same is her job. I'm not surprised that she's thought of trying something new."

He looked out the side window. "She's dating Ed! It seems to me like that would be weird enough for her! I must be getting too old for this job. Maybe all of that would've made sense to me ten years ago."

"I think that would've made sense to you ten *months* ago." Sharyn headed towards the heart of town that bordered Diamond Mountain Lake.

The area was still dominated by the smaller clapboard houses put up by the cotton mills fifty years ago for their workers. There were still a few more expensive estates from the 1920s when Diamond Springs was a resort town for the rich. But in the last ten years, condominiums and upper middle class, single-family homes began to dot the mountain slopes that were mirrored by the lake. Clint Walker's address on his license put him in one of the nicer, middle-class neighborhoods.

"Are you saying I'm not doing a good job anymore?"

"I didn't say that. Even totally unfocused and continually in a bad mood, you're a better deputy than you should be. You should've been a great sheriff."

"And we both know what I think about *that* idea." He looked down at the copy of the fax he held. "Am I really as bad as all that?"

"Worse." She saw the street they were looking for and turned right. "You're older than me. I was just being polite."

"There it is." He pointed out the two-story redbrick house. "Just being polite, huh? If you were still *just* T Raymond's daughter and not the sheriff, I'd tear up your behind for sassing me."

She laughed at him. "It's a good thing I'm the sheriff then, huh?"

They parked on the street and walked up to the house to ring the doorbell.

"Nice place. Wonder what Walker did for a living." Ernie looked around at the elaborate garden that surrounded the well-kept house.

Sharyn followed his gaze past the silver Lexus parked outside the garage. "Whatever it was, I guess he was pretty good at it."

"Not like me?" Ernie commented quickly as the door started to open.

"Yes?" The portly woman standing in the doorway took an immediate protective stance, folding her arms across her chest. She was dressed in an expensive, emerald-green business suit. Her dark red hair was a bouffant cloud around her heavily made-up face.

"Mrs. Walker?" Ernie took out his badge. "I'm Deputy Watkins. This is Sheriff Howard. We're looking for Clint Walker. Is he home?"

The woman's hazel eyes moved frantically back and forth between the two officers on her doorstep. Then they rolled back in her head and she fainted on the floor in front of them.

"It's gonna be that kind of day." Ernie knelt beside her.

Sharyn dialed 9-1-1. "Yeah, I noticed that."

LADONNA WALKER CAME to her senses with several paramedics hovering over her. She was still in her foyer. She pushed the paramedics away with an impatient hand, refusing to let them start an IV. "Go away! I'm fine! What's going on?"

Ernie stepped up and replied, "You fainted, ma'am. We just wanted to make sure that you were all right."

She struggled to her feet, despite the paramedics telling her to take it easy. "I'm not a baby! And I don't faint. I don't know what happened. Maybe something knocked me over. But I assure you, I didn't faint."

The lead paramedic shrugged and closed his medical bag. "You seem okay, Mrs. Walker. But it wouldn't hurt to contact your doctor. People just don't pass out for no reason."

"But people *do* pass out from shock." Sharyn moved forward. "If you're sure you're okay, Mrs. Walker, maybe we could have a talk."

The woman looked at her and patted her hair. "I have some appointments this afternoon, Sheriff. Maybe tomorrow."

The paramedics had Mrs. Walker sign some papers saying that she'd refused treatment. They packed up their equipment and prepared to move the stretcher they'd brought in with them.

"This can't wait, ma'am. It would be better for you to postpone those appointments." Ernie held the door for the medical personnel.

"Well, I never!" Ladonna Walker allowed her glacial stare to move from Ernie to Sharyn and back again.

"I won't be told what to do by a civil servant. You're supposed to work *for* me."

"We actually work to *protect* you, Mrs. Walker," Sharyn informed her. "And in this case, we're here to inquire about your husband."

"What about him?"

"Is he here?"

Mrs. Walker's chin raised a fraction higher above her blouse collar. "No, he's not. He's out of town on business. Why? Has he done something wrong?"

Ernie glanced around the elaborately decorated foyer. "When was the last time you saw him, ma'am?"

"Are you going to arrest him?"

"No, ma'am."

"Then I don't see that's any of your business, Deputy." She walked to the door and held it open. "I'm a very busy woman."

Sharyn didn't move. "If you won't answer our questions here, Mrs. Walker, we'll have to ask you to come to our office."

"Am I under arrest then, Sheriff?"

"No, ma'am."

Ladonna Walker turned to her marble-topped side table and scribbled on a piece of lavender-scented paper. She tore it free from the pad and handed it to Sharyn. "Here's my attorney's number. If you have any questions, I suggest you contact him."

Ernie started to speak, but Sharyn stopped him. "All right. Thank you, Mrs. Walker. We'll be in touch."

The woman made a loud *humphing* sound and stood

beside the door again. She slammed it shut as soon as they passed through it. They could hear the lock fall into place behind them.

Ernie whistled. "What do you think *that* was all about?"

"If I didn't know better, I'd think she was the one who put her husband in that car."

"But you know better, right?"

"Well, not yet. But that just seems too easy. I'd like to think it would be that simple, but *I* know better."

He took out his cell phone and called the office. "Trudy, will you ask Cari to see what she can find on Ladonna Walker, too?"

"You know," Sharyn reminded him, "you're going to have to talk to Cari. You work together. You can't go on pretending she's not there and giving Trudy messages for her. I was hoping you two sorted all of this out at the diner."

"Could we talk about the murder case, please? I'm too unfocused to deal with more than one subject at a time."

"Fine. Let's swing by the morgue and see if they have anything else for us. I feel like I'm walking around in the dark without a flashlight."

They drove in companionable silence through the late afternoon crowd that was spilling out of office buildings and rushing to appointments. The bright spring sunshine was beginning to open the pink azaleas that were in dozens of yards around town. Pale green leaves were sprouting on the slopes of the Uwharrie Mountains, creating a lush backdrop.

Ernie smiled up at them. "You know, last fall I didn't know if there'd be a single living thing left up there after the fires. But just look at it."

She looked up at Diamond Mountain, the tallest in the ancient range. It was only about 1,500 feet, nothing like the Smokies or even the Blue Ridge. But it was like a friendly giant that protected the town. At least, that's the way she grew up thinking about it. "I guess nature always finds a way to come back. Even from something as terrible as those forest fires. People are like that, too, you know."

"Don't get metaphorical on me. If you've got something to say about me and Annie, just come right out with it. You know I hate that stuff. And you're not good at it!"

She laughed as she turned into the hospital parking lot. "I was wrong. You're totally focused. Just not on your work. So since you brought it up, have you tried to talk to Annie about it?"

He waited until she pulled up the parking brake then put on his hat. "What can I say to her? I cheated on her. I called off our wedding. I don't know what else there is to say."

Sharyn left her hat in the car. She wasn't overly fond of it anyway, and the spring breeze felt good fluttering through her hair. Technically, it was lunchtime and she wasn't *necessarily* operating in her official capacity. She didn't have to wear her complete uniform.

They argued about Ernie's problem with Annie as they walked down the stairs and into the freezing basement beneath Diamond Springs Memorial Hospital. At different points in time, the basement had been used as a bomb shelter, a bootlegger's hideout, and a munitions depot during the Civil War. Now it was the county morgue and the crime scene lab.

Nick looked up from behind his desk as they walked into his office. They caught him with his mouth stuffed full of cheese—peanut butter crackers.

"What's for lunch?" Ernie asked. "Not Nabs again!"

"That's all they let us eat around here. We don't get real food." Nick took a drink of cold coffee. "Unless the beautiful lady sheriff makes us dinner."

"I already invited you. You don't have to suck up." She snatched one of his crackers. "You're lucky you get to eat at all."

Ernie took the last cracker. "Yeah. The beautiful *lady* sheriff doesn't let me eat at all. Or have any peace. Or any say-so in the department. Be glad you don't have to spend all day with her!"

She ignored him and focused on Nick. "We just had an interesting meeting with Mr. Walker's wife. She took one look at us and passed out cold."

"Really?" He swallowed the last of his coffee before they took that, too. "Was she still alive?"

Ernie shrugged. "I'm not so sure. The woman was like ice! I think she seemed like the type who could bury a man alive."

Nick got up and tossed the coffee cup into the garbage. "Well, that settles that. She's guilty. Do I still have to complete the autopsy?"

"I thought you liked that stuff." Ernie sniffed around on the big desk for anything else to eat.

"Not right at the end of the term. I'm teaching three psyche classes and two in forensics. That means five sets of finals, term papers and hundreds of whining students who want to know why they aren't going to get credit for this semester."

Sharyn smiled at him. "Sorry our murder doesn't fit your schedule. Since Commissioner Richmond likes you so much, maybe you could ask her for a raise and give up your teaching job."

"Julia gave me what she could to add to our fine high-tech forensics lab, and to hire my two worthy assistants. I wouldn't want to ask her for anything else right now. Besides, we go for months sometimes without needing any crime scene work. What would I do in between?"

"I heard the Richmond family is looking for a summer pool man," she teased him. "You'd look good in a tank top and shorts, holding one of those long bug nets."

Nick shuddered. "I don't do tank tops or shorts. But I heard there was a full-time vacancy in the sheriff's department. I suppose I could apply for that. I already know how to shoot a gun. Would I still have to wait six weeks before I could carry one?"

Ernie's mustache twitched. "Rules are rules. Unless the sheriff decides to apply her own rules. Then who knows what happens?"

"Well," Nick paused for effect. "I was just thinking about Marvella and how she wasn't supposed to carry a gun for six weeks but she managed to shoot the suspect in that last murder case. I could do that."

Sharyn shook them both off. "If we could move on to the case in hand, I'd appreciate it. Both of you need some focus. What do you have for us, Nick?"

He pulled on his lab coat. "Well, Sheriff, behind door number two, we have a man who has been dead at least five years. It could be anywhere from two weeks to two months before we have positive ID that the man is Clint Walker. And that will be if we get lucky and find some way to locate medical records and we don't need any DNA work from the state crime lab. I got an email yesterday telling me to expect long waits for forensic answers. They're short-handed."

"What about fingerprints?" Ernie nudged him.

"I'd show you why we don't have fingerprints," Nick replied with a gracious smile. "But the sheriff is a little squeamish about these things."

Sharyn pulled on a spare lab coat from the rack near the door and snapped on gloves. "I think you can show us whatever we need to see, Dr. Thomopolis."

He shrugged broad shoulders beneath the white coat. "There was that bear attack…"

"Never mind that. Lead the way."

Ernie put on a coat and gloves. He smiled but didn't look at his partner.

Nick clicked on the light in the lab, then pulled back the lab sheet for them to view the remains. "All that's really left is a little tissue and bones. The bottom half of him dried a little more in the car than in the dirt. We could probably get someone from Charlotte to do reconstruction if we can't find any other way to ID him. That's expensive. But at least we could see if his face matches the picture on his driver's license."

Sharyn put her hand to her throat but didn't back away from the corpse. She hated this part of the job but was steadily improving in her reaction to it. The first time she'd worked with Nick, she'd thrown up all over the lab. It was one of the most embarrassing moments of her life.

"We know that he wasn't killed by the two gunshots," Nick pointed out.

"He was shot twice and still died from something else?" Ernie peered at what was left of the body.

"Apparently. It's possible either one could've killed him after a while. One of them was lodged in his sternum. The other nicked his rib but not close to the heart. He could've bled to death if nothing else. But neither bullet was fatal on impact. He probably suffocated. From his position in the car, I'd say whoever shot him *thought* he was dead and started to bury the car. He rolled down the window and tried to get out. But the wall of dirt must've been pushed into place too quickly. He died trying to claw his way out."

The three of them stood quietly around the body, picturing the image in their minds. It wasn't a good way to die.

Sharyn shook herself away from her thoughts. "What about the bullets?"

"They're intact. I haven't had time to check yet. I should be able to do that today."

"How about the car?" Ernie pushed forward. "Anything on that yet?"

"We're not finished with it. They haven't even moved it from the cemetery. There are a lot of possibilities for evidence." Nick covered the remains. "But because everything has been exposed to the elements, it's going to take some time. We've lifted some prints from the interior but I'm still trying to find Clint Walker's prints, so I have something to compare them to. So far, what we've got hasn't come up on any database."

"If you could get them to look for a registration or license plate, it could help make the case that this *is* Clint Walker." Sharyn took off her gloves and facemask as she walked out of the room. "It may be a roundabout way of doing it but it would be better than nothing."

"Okay. I'll give them a call. From what they've told me, the interior of the car is in pretty good shape. They've found a few personal items. I *can* tell you that the car is a Mercedes. I don't know what make or year yet."

Ernie wrote it down. "Bad waste of a good car. Somebody really hated that boy to shoot him and then bury him alive."

"The killer might not have known he was still alive after he was shot," Sharyn said. "And probably didn't expect anyone to find him in their lifetime."

"I know what you're thinking," Ernie said. "I'll give Mrs. Walker's lawyer a call."

Nick brought out some plastic bags. "I haven't had a

chance to go over this stuff yet. We were lucky the car stopped some of the decay. This is his wallet and everything I found inside. He was wearing some expensive cuff links and a good watch that we found in the dirt."

Sharyn and Ernie looked through the contents of the wallet spread out in the plastic bags. Obviously, there was no robbery involved with the crime. Walker's wallet contained almost a thousand dollars in cash and several major credit cards. There were also pictures of two children. There was no writing on the backs of the photos and the images were faded.

"Definitely a boy and a girl." Ernie looked over Sharyn's shoulder.

Nick pointed to another photo. "Is that the woman you interviewed?"

She couldn't tell for sure. "It could be. But it's hard to say from this photo. I suppose we could have them touched up. The boy looks like he could be a younger teenager. The girl looks older. That was a long time ago. They'd be adults now."

Ernie looked at his watch. "Let's go back and see what Cari's dug up on this boy. If we get enough corroborating evidence, we don't have to go through all that DNA mess. He might be in bad shape, but a horse is still a horse, right?"

"Even with enough evidence to say the body *should* be Walker," Sharyn argued, "we'll have to do better than that. Right now, he could be anybody that someone wanted us to think was him. Including Walker himself, wanting to get away from his wife and kids."

Nick laughed and clapped Ernie on the back. "And on that note, I have to go back and grade more finals, otherwise I'm going to be having crackers and cold coffee for supper tonight."

"I'd find some way to get out of here for supper, if I were you," Ernie warned. "Standing a woman up once, even when a dead body's involved, is one thing. She's liable to shoot you if you try it again."

Sharyn kissed Nick's cheek. "Go ahead. I have to go anyway. I'll see you later."

"SO FAR," ERNIE SAID as they walked back out into the fading afternoon, "we have a fairly well-to-do man who had a nice house and kids. He drives off in his Mercedes one day and ends up buried alive."

"What does that tell you?"

"That I'm better off *not* being married?"

She frowned at him. "It tells me that his wife wasn't surprised that he was gone. Only that we *found* him."

He got into the Jeep and fastened his seat belt. "Yeah. That, too."

They started back down Main Street towards the courthouse. A shiny black Corvette cut them off then raced ahead, weaving in and out of the beginning of rush-hour traffic.

"Is he blind?" Ernie looked out his window at the car. "Or crazy?"

Sharyn turned on the flashing lights and siren. "Let's find out."

FOUR

Sharyn pursued the Corvette while Ernie checked on the plates to ID the car and driver.

"You're gonna love this," he told her. "The car is registered to David Matthews."

She didn't take her eyes from the crowded street as she followed the car past the courthouse to the old sheriff's office. "Nice toy. Roy must be paying him a lot more than I was."

"Maybe that's why Trudy wants to sign up with the police department." Ernie put the information into the laptop. "Now that I know, I think I'll talk to Roy about a job, too."

Sharyn slowed down and turned off the lights and siren as she realized that David was going to the office. "I think you were the one who just warned Nick about me shooting him. Don't tempt me."

They pulled into the parking lost as David was getting out of the car. Charlie was at the gate, watching them with a keen eye.

Ernie got out of the Jeep before Sharyn finished parking it. He yelled at David as the younger man was about to walk into the office.

"Hey, Ernie. What's up?"

"What's up? Do you know how fast you were driving down Main Street? We clocked you at sixty in a twenty zone."

David grinned at him. "Yeah, this baby will really fly."

"That's not all that's about to fly." Ernie took out his ticket book. "I already know your license number and your driving record. Let's just fly right to this ticket I'm about to give you for speeding and reckless driving."

"Aw, Ernie, cops don't give other cops tickets. Look, I was late for work and I didn't realize how fast I was going. Okay?"

Sharyn reached them just as Roy stumbled out of the office. They glared at each other a moment before nodding and going to stand behind their officers.

"What seems to be the problem, Deputy?" the police chief demanded.

"Officer Matthews here was pretending his shiny new car was an airplane," Ernie explained without looking up from the ticket book. "I was explaining to him that Main Street's not a runway."

The Chief exchanged dismal glances with his sergeant. "I appreciate you telling me, Deputy. But save your ticket. The police department handles speeding on the streets of Diamond Springs now. You'll have to catch him *outside* the city limits."

"I don't think the commission meant that the sheriff's department is supposed to stand by while a crime takes place in town," Sharyn told him. "Especially when

a reckless driver cuts me off and weaves through pe-
destrian traffic."

"He's a moron," Roy admitted. "No wonder you
didn't mind giving him up."

"Chief!" David looked embarrassed.

"Go on inside, Matthews. We'll talk about this later."

"Not before I hand him this ticket." Ernie ripped the
paper from the pad.

Roy intercepted the ticket and tore it to shreds before
he stuffed it into his pocket. "Your citations don't mean
anything here, Deputy. Why don't you go on down to
your little office in the basement?"

Ernie jumped forward. His fist connected with Roy's
square jaw. The Chief's head snapped back but his left
hook took Ernie by surprise, hitting him in the eye.

Sharyn tried to pull Ernie off Roy while David tried
to pull his boss away. Charlie came down from the
guardhouse but stayed carefully away from the flailing
arms and legs. Hearing the ruckus, deputies and officers
came running into the parking lot. The streetlights were
beginning to come on, illuminating the fight.

It took Sharyn, Ed and Joe to pull Ernie's wiry frame
away from the Chief's heavy-set one. A group of young
police officers held Roy back when he tried to get at
Ernie again. By the time it was over, Marvella and JP
had arrived for the nightshift. The usually empty parking lot was full of shouting and swearing.

Charlie inserted himself between the groups. "Now
all of you settle down! I think you got as good as you

gave. So go on! Go about your business! I'd hate to call the highway patrol to settle this."

Everyone knew Charlie. He'd been a part of the sheriff's department before Roy or Ernie joined. His gruff voice brought them to their senses, and the two groups took their fighters to their respective corners.

"What happened?" Ed demanded, looking at Ernie's battered face.

Sharyn gave him a brief explanation as she sent Marvella to get some ice.

Ed was David's uncle. He'd been embarrassed enough by the boy's behavior when he was with the sheriff's department. When he left to become a police officer, he wasn't sure whether to be happy he was gone or mad because he left. Right now, he was just plain mad. "I'll take care of this."

"No more!" Sharyn deterred him. "Just let it settle, please. You going out and kicking David's butt won't help matters. We have to work together, whether we like it or not."

Ernie shrugged aside the ice pack that Marvella tried to hold on his face. "I'm going home. You people do what you want."

Cari rushed to his side. "You should go to the emergency room, Ernie. He might've broken something."

"I've been hit harder by accident." He glared at her then left the office.

Sharyn took a deep breath. Marvella shrugged and went to put the ice pack away.

"This is all my fault." Cari's big blue eyes held un-shed tears. "He did this because of me."

Marvella shook her head, her glossy black curls dancing around her handsome dark face. "It's not your fault, honey. The man only has himself to blame. And he's the only one who can dig himself out of this mess."

Ed grumbled as he left for the night. Joe told Sharyn that he'd go and check on Ernie.

"I don't understand," Deputy JP Santiago complained. "What goes on here during the day? Marvella and I don't have these problems."

Sharyn smiled at him. "Be glad you don't. We got a call from the highway patrol about an accident just off the Interstate. They think an eighteen-wheeler might have flipped off a bridge near Frog Meadow."

JP nodded to her. "Yes, ma'am. We'll head over that way."

"Thanks. I appreciate you not giving me a hard time."

His swarthy face was aghast. "When have I ever given you a hard time, Sheriff? Tell me and I swear it won't happen again."

She amended her words. "You're a good man, JP. I just wanted you to know how much I appreciate you being here and *not* giving me a hard time."

His black eyes shone. "Oh! Thanks. Sometimes, I'm not sure. But I try to do a good job so that you can have faith in me."

Marvella put on her hat, wound a pink scarf around her neck then scooted him away from Sharyn. "Yeah, she knows you love your job, honey. Now, let's get a move on. I want to be back in time for Jay Leno. He's having Whitney Houston on his show tonight. They say she's lost weight again. What I could tell that child she's doing wrong!"

Sharyn sat down beside Cari when they were gone. "Marvella's right. What's happening with Ernie doesn't have anything to do with you. He'll get his head screwed back on at some point."

Cari wiped a tear from her cheek. "I found some information for you about Clint Walker." She handed Sharyn the stack of paper. "If you wouldn't mind, I'd like to go home now."

"Sure. That's fine. I'm going to take this home with me anyway. I'll see you tomorrow."

SHARYN HURRIED BACK to her apartment to change clothes and heat up the pasta. But for once, Nick was early. He was sitting on her steps with a bottle of wine in one hand and a bouquet of spring flowers in the other.

"I can't believe you're here already." She opened the door and let him inside.

"I'm happy to see you, too." He put the wine and flowers on the cabinet. "I thought I'd come early since the explanation for where you were all day is going to take so long."

She closed the door behind them and went to the refrigerator to take out the pasta. "I'm going to pretend you're not here yet. Otherwise, the whole evening will be spoiled."

"Is it okay if I watch TV while you're ignoring me? They interviewed me today about the guy in the Mercedes. You know how I like to see myself on television."

She laughed as she went into the bedroom and closed the door behind her. Nick hated being interviewed. He'd actually adopted disguises to get away from overzealous reporters.

It was too cool for her new sundress so she took out a long black skirt she'd bought at the same time. She was looking for a blouse to go with it and trying to do something with her hair when the doorbell rang. "Nick? Will you get that?"

She finally found a lightweight blue sweater. She was on the floor, hunting frantically for her only pair of dress shoes, when the bedroom door opened. She scrambled to her feet. She couldn't believe Nick would just walk in.

But it wasn't him. It was her mother.

"What are you doing in here while Nick is out there starving to death?" Faye Howard's dulcet tone chimed across the room as she walked in followed by a cloud of L'air du Temps. "I wouldn't leave him waiting too long, if I were you. And what were you doing on the floor?"

Sharyn glanced through the open doorway, glad that she'd already changed clothes. "I was looking for shoes. What brings you by?" *And when are you leaving?*

"Caison and I were on our way out to dinner when we heard about the man in the car. I wanted to come by and make sure that you were all right."

Sharyn could hear ex-senator Caison Talbot laughing with Nick in the next room. She'd planned for this evening for so long but apparently, nothing was going to work out with it. "I'm fine. Thanks for stopping by."

"You know, I remember Clint Walker. He was quite a hunk. I danced with him once at a charity ball." Faye preened in the vanity mirror. She patted her blond hair even though not a single strand was out of place. She licked her finger and smoothed it over a carefully arched brow. "You father was pretty jealous."

Sharyn couldn't imagine her father being jealous of anyone, but she *could* imagine her mother wanting to think he was. She was still a high school beauty queen at heart. "Maybe you could help us out with some details about Mr. Walker. We're having a hard time with his wife."

Faye spritzed on a little more perfume. "I'd be glad to. If I were Ladonna, I'd be upset, too. She's a good woman and she's had a hard life. You know, I always wondered what happened to him."

"Well, I'd appreciate whatever you could tell us about him." *But not tonight.*

"Of course, darling. We'd be glad to stay and talk shop. I'll just have Caison call the restaurant and cancel the reservations."

Sharyn grabbed her before she could leave the room. "Maybe we could do it tomorrow. I could buy you lunch."

Her mother's eyes widened with understanding. "Of *course!* I'm sorry. Whatever you have to do to get Nick to marry you."

"It's just dinner, Mother." Sharyn hoped Nick didn't hear her mother's remark. "But thanks for understanding."

Faye hugged her daughter then swept regally back out to find Caison. "We have to go. Nick and Sharyn are going to have a *special* dinner. *Alone.*"

Talbot got to his feet easily. He'd dropped about thirty pounds since his heart attack the previous year. But his full head of white hair still made him distinctive. He was back to practicing law again, after losing his senate seat to Jack Winter. "I understand. Good luck, young man."

Nick shook his hand and glanced at Sharyn. "Thanks, sir. I'm sure I'll need it."

Faye was actually giggling as the couple walked out the door to their waiting limousine. Sharyn looked out of the window at them, wishing she could get Caison to answer a few questions about her father and Jack. But that wasn't going to happen. He was as cryptic as the black book she'd found, and as slippery as Jack.

"I think the pasta's ready." Nick stirred the slightly overdone ziti in the pot.

She pulled out the salad and turned on the oven to warm the bread. "Maybe you could open the wine before any other disaster happens."

They sat down together at the table. She lit the candles and he poured the wine.

"Now are you going to tell me where you went?"

She spooned out some ziti and put it on his plate. "It's not as big a deal as you're making it out to be."

"If you didn't want me to make a big deal about it, sweetheart, you shouldn't have kept me guessing all day. Did you have to go to traffic court or something? They finally found those old parking tickets?"

Sharyn finally gave in and told him about the phone call from Skeeter Johnson and her trip to Raleigh.

"There." He spooned some grated cheese on his pasta. "That wasn't so hard, was it?"

"He told me that Jack was responsible for my father's death."

"But didn't give you any proof. I think he was just looking for a way out."

"You don't think it's possible?"

He stared at her across the table. "Sharyn, the man is a killer and a liar. If this is true, why didn't he say it at the trial?"

"What if it was *your* father, Nick? Wouldn't you want to know the truth?"

"Not if it meant that something bad could happen because of it. No matter what you find out, it won't bring your father back. It won't erase the pain of his death."

She played with the pasta on her plate, suddenly not hungry. "No. But it might bring Jack to justice."

Nick took a sip of wine and studied the glass. His dark eyes were serious in the candlelight. "That's what this is *really* all about, isn't it? Getting Jack. You're obsessed with him. I don't know if I should be jealous or worried about your sanity."

They'd had this discussion before. "I've told you. I'm

the sheriff. I'm supposed to bring down the bad guys. That's all he is to me."

"He's also a state senator. You're closer to being arrested as a criminal than he is. Let it go."

"I can't."

The silence was suddenly overwhelming between them. The smell of burning bread brought Sharyn to her feet.

Nick took the oven mitt from her when someone knocked at the door. "It's *your* door. I don't even like to answer my own."

Ernie was standing in the hall. He was carrying a single satchel and a sleeping bag. "Now don't make a big deal out of this. I just couldn't take the salsa music coming from the restaurant anymore. I don't need a bed and I'll eat all my meals at the diner."

Sharyn looked at his swollen, bruised face and threw her arms around him. "It's okay. We'll work it out. For once, let *me* help you."

He hugged her tightly. "Yeah, I guess I'm just going through a bad patch."

Nick looked at his pager. "Hi, Ernie. I hate to almost eat and run but I just got buzzed. I'll see the two of you later."

"Don't let me run you off." Ernie saw the candles and the bottle of wine on the table. "I don't want to ruin anybody else's love life."

"Not much here to ruin." Nick put on his jacket. "Your face looks like it went through a meat grinder. You probably need a few stitches over that eye."

"I've had worse. I'm just going to go over here and find a place for my sleeping bag."

Sharyn could've stepped outside with Nick but she wasn't sure what else there was to say. She was angry and hurt that he didn't take this discovery more seriously. She looked up into his handsome face and somber gaze. "I guess I'll see you tomorrow."

"Yeah. I guess so."

"Good night. Sorry about the ziti and the bread. The wine was good."

He kissed her forehead. "Let's not do this again. I had more fun in the morgue today."

She watched him go down the stairs then went back into her apartment, closed the door and locked it. So much for their romantic dinner together.

"I'm sorry. I didn't mean to cause trouble between you two." Ernie inspected his sleeping bag for non-existent holes.

She sat in the chair beside him. "It wasn't you. It was the ghost of Jack Winter. Even when he's in Raleigh, he's ruining my life."

"But you know Nick and I are both right. And you know your daddy would tell you the same thing if he was here. Some time, some place, that snake will step wrong and somebody will put him out of our misery. Until then, you don't have anything on him. And he's not gonna let you get anything, either."

"Nick thinks I'm infatuated with Jack. I think he believes all of that stuff the papers said last winter about Jack and I having a relationship."

Ernie sighed. "Nick's a man in a tough spot. He's in love with a woman who goes out of her way to risk her life every day. He wants to protect you. But he knows he can't. Give him some credit, Sharyn. He's not stupid. He knows you hate Jack. He just wishes you could do it from the sidelines. Unfortunately, we both know you better."

For a moment, she was tempted to tell him about the book she found behind the panel in her old office. But she knew his protective attitude would color that, as well. She needed time to figure out what was written in the book. Right now, it was just a lot of squiggly lines. Once she knew if it was something important, she could tell Ernie. And Nick.

She got up from the chair and changed the subject. "I'd better get this mess cleaned up. I guess I'm never going to be much of a cook. If I ever have anyone over for dinner again, I'm going to get takeout."

"Let me help you. The cooking thing doesn't matter so much. I'm a better cook than Annie. But even her boiled water is better than my favorite gourmet meal. I know you wouldn't believe it by my actions, but I really love that woman."

Sharyn let him rinse the dishes and clean off the table. She put the rest of the ziti and the scorched bread in the garbage. "I know you love her. And I know she loves you. What happened with Cari was stupid, no doubt about it. And you should've known better."

"You can't tell me anything I haven't told myself over and over. Those were some long nights at the

Motel Six." He handed her the last plate and wiped off the table.

"Do you remember when I was in the hospital after Skeeter Johnson almost shot off my kneecap? I was ready to give up being sheriff. I'd done something so stupid and so reckless that I didn't think I could ever look at you or Joe or Ed without feeling like an idiot."

He paused beside her at the sink. "I remember. And I know I said some tough things to you, but you got up out of that bed the next week and came back to work. Everyone thought you were too green for the job. They gave you a hard time. But you stuck it out."

"Let me reciprocate. Go back to Annie. Crawl on you hands and knees if you have to. You loved each other when you were kids, then were separated. Don't let it happen again. You don't have another thirty years to wait for her. Don't be even more stupid and let a few minutes with Cari ruin both of your lives."

He digested her words. "Nope. It just doesn't have the same impact. I guess you're not old enough yet."

She dried her hands on a dish towel. "That's funny. Aunt Selma was just asking me last week if I thought she should go away for the weekend with Sam."

"Is that going to be Uncle Sam at some point?"

"No!" She grimaced. "He's still just going to be Sam to me."

"Maybe I should go out there and give Sam a run for his money. Selma's still a mighty fine-looking woman."

Sharyn took his hand and looked into his eyes. "Go back to Annie. Otherwise, I'll shoot you in the foot and the two of you can get back together in the hospital because she feels sorry for you and you can't work."

"You think that would work?"

"I think if you keep being impossible to work with, I won't have any choice."

"Okay. Now can we talk about you and Nick? Because I have a bunch of clever things to say about your relationship that *will* have an impact. And I won't even have to resort to threatening to shoot you. I'm better than that."

"I'm going to change clothes and then I'm going to look at all the information that Cari found about Mr. Walker and his family. The information that you're going to thank her for tomorrow *personally*."

"You're right about that. I owe her an apology. Is she still dating that assistant DA?"

"As far as I know," she answered. "I never knew being sheriff meant keeping up with your deputies' love lives. I guess I should've interned with Dear Abby."

She thought about Nick while she was changing clothes. The black T-shirt and sweatpants she put on reflected her mood. Maybe he was right. Maybe she was obsessed with Jack. The man *was* in her thoughts a lot.

He'd insinuated himself into her life by one means or another the last few years. First, trying to intimidate her as DA, then actually making romantic overtures to her. He'd dated her mother, sneaked into her house, haunted her every move.

Now, he was hundreds of miles away but she was still thinking about him. It was like being trapped in a game of chess with someone she knew was slightly better at it than her. She wasn't sure she could win this game. But she knew she had to keep trying.

It was almost midnight when Sharyn finished reviewing the last page of information that Cari had found about Clint Walker. She handed it to Ernie, got up and stretched. Her eyes were starting to daze and her brain was still processing the information. She was tired but she didn't think she could sleep. "I can't do anything else tonight. I'm going out for a walk. I'll see you in the morning."

He looked up at her. "Want some company?"

"Not really. I prowl best alone, thanks. Don't sleep out here on the floor. I have that whole other room."

"Okay, thanks. But I don't know if I can sleep in Faye's old room. There's too many flowers and such."

She slipped her arms into her hooded jacket. "I think you should try. I'm likely to step on you if you're out here on the floor all night."

"Doesn't seem like there's going to be much of a night left by the time you come back. You know, you have to get some rest." Ernie picked up his satchel and walked towards the spare bedroom.

"If I wanted to live with my mother, I would've moved back with her after they finished repairing the house," she warned him. "You can stay as long as you don't nag me about my bad habits."

He scratched his chin. "That's a two-way street, Sheriff. Maybe we should have something like a cuss jar. That way, when we break the rules like you know we will, we'll have to put money in. You know neither one of us is good at keeping our opinions to ourselves."

"Yeah, that's true. But I guess it's better than salsa music. I'll see you later." She locked the door behind her then opened the door to the street, almost falling over an obstacle on the steps. "What are you doing out here?"

"Waiting for you," Nick answered. "Like always."

She sat down beside him. The breeze from the lake was cold on her face as she stared at the crescent moon that hung low in the sky above them. "How long have you been out here?"

"I'm not sure. I went home and changed clothes and took off my watch. I think that old church down the street was chiming nine when I walked up."

"Why didn't you come upstairs?"

"I knew you and Ernie were talking. I knew you'd be out here sooner or later. Everyone knows you stalk the streets of Diamond Springs at night. All you need is a mask and a cape."

She put her hands into her pockets. "Are you spying on me?"

"I don't have to. Everyone knows you. Everyone knows I'm seeing you. So everyone tells me everything you do that could possibly make me have a heart attack. I'm not as young as I seem."

Sharyn laughed and stood up. The stairs were too cold to sit for long. "You've always seemed pretty old to me. When I was finishing school, I thought you were the same age as Ernie and my father."

"Thanks. You always know just what to say."

"It's a knack. Want to go for a walk by the lake, old man?"

He got slowly, deliberately, to his feet and hunched over a little. "I think I could manage that. Although I can't promise not to mention your obsession with Jack."

She sighed and took his hand as they started walking. "I know. I can live with that. If you can live with knowing that I have to do what I think is right."

He squeezed her hand gently. "As long as you can live with me worrying about you while you're doing what you think is right."

"This could go on all night." She moved closer to him and he put his arm around her. "Let's change the subject. Who was that call from that you got at dinner?"

"Oh, yeah. Let's talk about work. Safe subject. But in this case, I lied. No one really called me. I just used it as a convenient excuse. It was a miracle that no one called either of us. We managed to ruin dinner all by ourselves."

"I can't believe you lied to me. I've shot men for less."

He hugged her closer. "I'll show you mine if you'll show me yours."

"Don't get me started on your gun collection. It's bad enough that I know you have more guns than the sheriff's office. If we ever have a terrorism alert, I'll have to detain you for it."

They walked silently for a while. The sweet smell of new spring growth and lake water drifted by them. It was downhill from Sharyn's apartment to the lake. The moon danced across Diamond Mountain, reflected in the still, clear water.

They stood with their arms wrapped around each other for a long time. A few mournful owls called from the trees around the lake. Most of the houses were dark at the edges of the water. Empty, covered boats bobbed at the marina.

"I'm not really jealous of Jack as long as I'm the one standing *here* with you," he whispered in her ear.

She kissed his cheek. "You're right. I'm obsessed with him. But nothing like I'm obsessed with you."

He kissed her, his lips lingering on hers, their warm breaths mingling.

"Sheriff! *Yoo-hoo!* Sheriff!"

Sharyn reluctantly looked up. "Did you change your voice?"

"The question should be—when did I have time to become a ventriloquist?"

"*Yoo-hoo!* It's me, Sheriff. Nan Bellows. Remember me? We worked together on that murder case a few years back."

Sharyn squinted out at the water. She finally saw the old fishing boat. She remembered Nan from her childhood as well as from "working together" when they finally took Captain Billy Bost's plane out of Diamond Mountain Lake. "Hi, Nan. How are you?"

"Just fine, like always. Just doin' a piece of night

fishing. Them crappies is biting good tonight. Want to catch a few? I used to take you and your daddy out once in a while, remember?"

"I remember. I don't think I'm up for fishing tonight though. Thanks anyway."

Nan's laughter floated out to the shore. "I suppose I can see that. You're fishin' for something else tonight. Who's that with you? I hope you ain't breaking that fine young corpse doctor's heart?"

Sharyn and Nick both laughed. They couldn't actually make out the woman's face on the boat but they could hear her perfectly.

"See? I told you," Nick reminded Sharyn. "You can't go anywhere or do anything without someone thinking about me."

"Oh, are you the fine *young* corpse doctor?"

"Yeah. That's me. And that's why I specialized in forensics instead of pediatrics. I might have some trouble getting patients with that title."

Sharyn yelled back to Nan. "No, I'm not breaking his heart tonight. I'll see you later. Good luck with your fishing."

They were standing close enough together to feel both of their pagers vibrate at the same time.

"Well, that's enough intimacy for tonight." Nick moved to check his pager.

Sharyn looked at hers, too. "I think we're both going to the same place. Want a ride?"

FIVE

THE 9-1-1 CALL came in from a small home east of Clara-ville. It was about twenty minutes up the Interstate from Diamond Springs. When Sharyn, Nick and Ernie arrived, the house and yard were ablaze with light.

"Well," Ernie said, "at least Roy's not here. There are still some parts of this county that have some respect for the sheriff's office."

Nick put on a pair of sterile gloves and looked around the yard. "Do you think it always looks like this?"

Marvella breezed up to them. "Don't thank me now. I just happened to have the spotlights in the trunk of the car. I thought we might need them to look for the perp."

Ernie folded his arms across his chest. "What is that around your neck?"

She pushed the hot-pink scarf back from her shoulder. "I needed something to make this *uniform* livable. I don't think a scarf is too much. Do you, JP?"

Her partner settled his hat farther down on his head. "No. You look very nice."

"Let's not have this discussion again, Marvella." Ernie stepped closer to her. "I don't want to see you wearing anything that isn't issued by the county when you're working."

She made a face at him as he walked past her. "I've been wearing this for a week. How come you haven't said something until now?"

"Because I didn't *see* it until now. But don't let me see it again. How many times do I have to tell you?"

"My underwear isn't issued by the county," she taunted him. "What do you want me to do about that?"

"Nothing, unless you plan to wear it on the outside of your uniform."

Sharyn ignored their exchange. Part of Ernie's job was handling issues with the deputies. Mostly, she let him do what he thought was best. She tried not to undermine his authority. "What's going on out here, JP? Are we looking for someone?"

"I don't know." He took out his notebook, his dark eyes grateful to be out of the other conversation. "We answered the nine-one-one call and found a woman dead inside this house. We surveyed the area but didn't see anyone except the woman who called us."

"How did she die?" Nick took out his cell phone. "Please tell me she was a hundred-and-two-years-old and died in her sleep."

JP's comfortable brown face was anxious. "I don't think so, sir. She looks much younger than that. And I think it might be the gunshot wound in her head that killed her. Sorry."

Sharyn patted his shoulder. "He was just kidding, JP. Wishful thinking."

Nick sighed. "Where is she?"

"That's very funny, sir. A very good joke."

"No. Really. Where is she in the house? Bedroom? Bathroom?"

"In the kitchen."

"Thanks, JP." Sharyn separated the two. "While the M.E. takes a look at her, let's talk to whoever called 9-1-1."

Marvella stepped forward. "Oh, she's in the back of the cruiser. I didn't want to take a chance on her getting away. I put up these lights in case she had help. *And* I checked her for blood and GSR just the way Nick said. She's clean."

Sharyn was impressed. Marvella might get on Ernie's nerves but she was shaping up to be a darn good deputy. "Okay. Let's go talk to her."

The petite woman in the car was on the verge of hysteria. She was in her slippers and robe. Her dark brown hair was wild on her head. "She called me. I rushed over. But I was too late. I might've been able to stop her."

Sharyn helped her out of the car. They sat on the front porch and talked while Nick and Ernie worked inside. "What was her name?"

"Vicky Rogers. We were friends all the way through school. We grew up together in Diamond Springs. She moved out here with her husband, Stan, last year."

"And you are?"

"Rosemarie Marshal." The woman stared at her like she'd seen a ghost. "Maybe I'm wrong? Maybe she's not dead, Sheriff. Will they check her for that? I mean, they won't just take her and stick her somewhere unless she's really dead, right?"

"They'll check her for that," Sharyn assured her. "You said she called you. What do you think happened?"

"She's been talking crazy for about a month now. Weird things. Talking about killing herself, how life isn't worth living. She called me tonight and told me that tonight was it. I begged her not to do it. I told her I was coming over. But I was too late. I can't believe it."

Ernie came to the screen door. "Sheriff? Could you step in here for a moment?"

Rosemarie began to sob—deep, gasping cries that seemed like they would tear her slender frame apart. Sharyn called 9-1-1 dispatch again and asked them where the paramedics were. She didn't want to leave the woman this way.

Dispatch told her they were about five minutes away. There was an emergency on the Interstate that had taken precedence over the first call. She thanked them and rounded up Marvella to sit with Rosemarie until they could get there.

Walking inside, she found Nick and Ernie kneeling beside a woman's body on the kitchen floor. There was blood all around her as well as on the white cabinets behind her. Her pale green robe was soaked in it. Sharyn could never get over how much blood pumped through the human body. "Does it look like a suicide?"

Nick rifled through his medical bag. "The gun was

still in her hand. It looks like she put the gun up to her temple like a lot of people do. There's GSR on her hand and the wound. That's the most I can tell you right now."

"I found a note." Ernie handled the paper carefully as he bagged it. "It reads like a suicide note."

Sharyn took a look at it. It was printed. Probably on the computer in the kitchen. The paper was clean and the note was short: *I can't live with this anymore. It's too much. I'm sorry. Please tell my family that I love them.*

"What do you think she was talking about?" Ernie read it again as she read it.

"I don't know. Let me see if her friend has any idea."

She walked back to the porch. Mrs. Marshal was still sitting in the same place. A paramedic unit, an ambulance and an unidentified pickup truck pulled into the yard. JP went to talk to the paramedics.

A man got out of the pickup and started towards the house. "What's going on?" He looked at all of the vehicles parked in the yard. "What's everybody doing here?"

Sharyn intercepted him. "Let's step over here. Are you Mr. Rogers?"

The man pushed the worn baseball cap back on his head. "Yeah. I'm Stan Rogers. Are you Sheriff Howard? What are you doing here? Is something wrong with Vicky?"

"Yes. I'm sorry, sir. I hate to have to tell you this way. Your wife is dead."

"What?"

"We believe Vicky committed suicide. It might be

better if you wait out here until they get everything sorted out."

"I don't believe it! Where is she? I just talked to her a few hours ago. She was fine. She wouldn't do a thing like this. Let me see her!"

"You're going to have to wait out here, sir." Sharyn restrained him. "I don't want this to be any harder on you than it has to be. But for both your sakes, we need to be sure what happened."

The paramedics were taking Rosemarie to the ambulance. She saw Stan and called out to him.

He ran towards her. "Rosie? Were you here? What happened?"

Sharyn let him go and stood aside while they talked. It might be a clear case of suicide, but listening and asking questions would put any doubts to rest.

"I wasn't here. She called me. I got here as soon as I could. It was awful seeing her laying there."

Stan was weeping. "But she didn't really kill herself, right, Rosie? She wouldn't do that. She'd *never* do a thing like that."

The paramedic signaled Sharyn and she drew Vicky's husband away from the stretcher. They put Rosemarie into the ambulance and took her to the hospital.

Stan looked at Sharyn. "How did she do it?"

She didn't pretend not to understand what he was asking. "She shot herself. I don't think she suffered."

He collapsed on the ground at her feet. The paramedics rushed over to him and asked Sharyn to step back while they treated him. There was nothing more she could do for him at that point.

The crime scene van had been in the yard for a few minutes without showing any sign of life. Nick had already yelled out a few times with no response. Megan and Keith were busy kissing. They didn't even see Sharyn until she knocked on the window a few times.

Megan finally rolled the window down. "Hey, Sheriff. Heard there was another dead person out here."

"She's in the house. Nick's already in there. He's been looking for you."

The two young people glanced at each other before jumping out of the van.

"What's he doing here so soon?" Keith ran to the back doors and threw them open. "He's never in a good mood when he's here first."

Sharyn watched them go from lethargy to lightning. "He came with me. I couldn't tell what kind of mood he was in."

Nick's bellow from the porch for the pair to hurry up answered their question.

Megan panted as she raced by Sharyn with an oversize bag. "Do me a favor, huh? Don't *ever* bring him with you again. I like it better when he's late!"

A second ambulance pulled up to transport the victim. The paramedics gave Stan Rogers some oxygen and offered him a sedative that he refused. He stayed on the damp ground even as rain began falling. Nothing could induce him to move.

"I'm sorry for your loss, Mr. Rogers." Sharyn put her poncho around him. "If there's anything I can do…"

Pain etched sharp angles on his thin face in the eerie light. "You could tell her father, Sheriff. I don't have the heart for it and he should know, I suppose."

"All right. How do I get in touch with him?"

"He's a retired admiral. George Vendicott. He lives about a mile down the road. She moved out here, after he had his stroke last year, to take care of him. But I guess she needed somebody to take care of her. If she'd waited a little while, I would've been home. We could've talked. I can't stand that she died alone out here."

Sharyn crouched down beside him and drew out the note in the plastic bag. "I hate to ask you this, but could you look at this note? Does it make any sense to you?"

He held the paper like it was a butterfly, too fragile to really touch. He read through the lines again and again. "No. I don't know what she's talking about. What does it mean, Sheriff?"

She took the note back from him. "I hope we can find out. In the meantime, do you have some place to stay while they finish up here?"

He told her that his sister lived a few miles away. Sharyn took JP aside and asked him to take Stan to his sister's farm *after* he checked him for blood and GSR. When the deputy looked surprised, she shrugged. Even suicides had to be investigated.

She went back into the house and watch Nick working for a few minutes. Marvella and Ernie were bagging the computer and keyboard to take into the office.

Someone would need to prove that the note came from the computer and what time it was written. "If you don't need me, I'm going down the road to inform Mrs. Rogers's father before he finds out about this on the morning news. I'll be back as soon as I can."

Ernie closed the plastic bag around the computer. "Go on. And go home after that and get some sleep. We'll finish up here. I can ride back with Marvella and JP."

"Okay, thanks. I'll see you in the morning. You can sleep in awhile if you need to. I'll call you if there's an emergency. And you don't have to go to the diner for breakfast. There's some food in the refrigerator. Help yourself."

Heads turned and ears perked up. Megan and Keith glanced at Nick for any sign of reaction. Marvella *tsked* but kept on working.

"I wish you would've waited to tell me that in private." Ernie rolled his eyes as he realized that *his* words made it worse. "For the record, I'm just staying with the sheriff for a while to get away from the Motel Six."

Marvella waved her hand. "Whatever."

Keith adjusted his glasses and whispered, "Sorry, Dr. Thomopolis." He knew what it was like to be dumped by one of the Howard women. Sharyn's younger sister, Kristie, was his steady for a while before deciding she could live without him.

Nick mumbled something, too engrossed in his work to pay much attention to what was being said, and told him to get back to work. His two assistants darted painful looks at the sheriff's back as she walked out the door.

Sharyn refused to get involved in a needless round of questions and answers about Ernie staying with her. She had more important things on her mind.

She'd met Admiral Vendicott during a previous investigation. He'd provided important information that helped her solve a fifty-year-old murder case. Knowing him didn't make her task any easier. It was always bad when she had to tell someone that a person they loved was dead. It never got any better. She never assigned the task to someone else unless she didn't have any choice. She wasn't sure if it was something a sheriff was required to do. She only knew it was right for her to do it.

She thought about the woman lying dead on her kitchen floor. Her husband seemed surprised and upset by the news of her suicide. The note was too brief to really provide much of a clue as to why she'd taken her own life. Maybe they'd find that it was a mental illness. It wouldn't ease the loss, but it might make some sense of it for them.

The rough gravel road was dark and deserted. Rain fell steadily as she drove towards the admiral's house. It would be daybreak soon. But for now, the only light came from the farmhouses she passed. There were no streetlights. This end of the county hadn't changed much in the past twenty years. Progress was slow to reach the outer farming areas that surrounded Diamond Springs. Once you left the city limits, there was no cable TV or garbage service. Pump houses in every yard showed that the county water system was still years away from reaching here.

Sharyn pulled into the driveway beside the small brick house. As she got out of the Jeep, the rain intensified the scent of white wisteria that grew along the side wall. She took a deep breath to settle her nerves, then went up to the door and knocked.

How many times had she brought terrible news to people with a single knock at their door? It always seemed to happen in the rain, during the night or early in the morning. She looked towards the east. The sky was starting to get light. A rooster crowed from somewhere behind the house. She was getting soaked waiting for the admiral to come to the door.

Finally, the porch light came on and the door scraped slowly open. She looked down the barrel of a shotgun pointed at her head.

"What do you want?" The man behind the gun was wearing a green plaid robe that was open around brown pajamas. He looked thin and fragile but his hand was steady on the gun.

"Admiral Vendicott? I'm Sheriff Sharyn Howard. We met a few years back." The sight of the gun pointed at her made her pulse race. But she didn't panic. It wasn't the first time she'd been met at the door with a shotgun. She was sure it was loaded. People out here didn't trust the law to protect them. And they didn't come to the door to meet a stranger with a gun that didn't fire.

Her words didn't mean anything to him. "Let me see some ID."

She held up her badge so that the light shone on it. "I'm sorry to disturb you at this hour, sir."

"Then what are you doing here? I'm an old man. You almost gave me a heart attack. What was so important you couldn't call in the morning?"

A trickle of rain ran down her back and made her shiver. She hoped he didn't see it and mistake the movement for a threat. "Please put the gun down, sir. I just need to talk to you."

He cocked the trigger. "I think you can say whatever you need to say from right where you are. Then I'll decide if I should put the gun down. I used to work for the government, you know. I know the kind of things that go on."

Sharyn didn't want to tell him this way but she also didn't want to fight him for the gun. "It's your daughter, sir. She committed suicide a few hours ago. I'm sorry."

"Vicky?" The gun shook. "Are you saying that Vicky's dead?"

The old man suddenly collapsed on the floor. Sharyn moved forward in time to catch the gun before it fell with him. But the old trigger didn't need any other prompting to make it fire. The shot roared past her ear and into the misty gray morning.

She forced herself to breathe, but her hands were shaking and her ears were ringing as she put the gun on the floor. She crouched down beside the old man, wondering if she should put in another call for an ambulance. "Are you all right, sir?"

"Of course I'm not all right, you idiot! You just told me my only child is dead. How do you expect me to feel?"

She took his arm and helped him into a chair, then sat across from him. He'd changed dramatically since she'd seen him last. The stroke had left him a bare skeleton. He was hardly able to stand. His head shook as he put his hands to his face and sobbed.

"I'm sorry. I meant, do you need medical attention?"

"No. I don't know why, but I'm still alive. It wasn't bad enough when my wife, Juanita, died. Now Vicky's dead, too. I'm completely alone. But my heart can't seem to break enough to stop this infernal existence."

"Did you know your daughter had any thoughts about suicide?" Sharyn changed the subject. She couldn't help him with the cross life had given him to bear. But maybe she could help him understand what happened to his daughter.

"Vicky is a Navy brat. She's tough. She'd never kill herself." He wiped his face on his robe. "How did she die?"

"She shot herself."

"That's ridiculous! My daughter is a sane, rational young woman. I didn't raise her to be a coward. She was murdered. This county has gone to the wolves since they elected that woman sheriff."

Sharyn ignored the remark. It wasn't the first time she'd heard grumbling about the sheriff. There *were* people who voted for Roy. "Do you have any reason to think that someone would murder Vicky?"

He pounded his hand on the side of his chair. "It was Stan, her useless husband! He was always jealous of our relationship. He didn't want to move out here. He was afraid he'd miss his precious football games. No ESPN, you know. You need to arrest him for killing my daughter!"

Duty bound to listen and record his remarks, Sharyn wrote them down. "I'll check this out, sir. I'll let you know what I find. You questioning her suicide makes this an official inquiry. There'll be an autopsy."

"Good! I don't want that skunk to get away with this. Put him in jail before he tries to get away."

"Is there someone I can call for you? Maybe someone who can come and stay with you?"

"I just told you that I'm alone in the world. Go on. Get some evidence on Stan. That's all you can do for me." He picked up his gun. "You're lucky I'm not ten years younger. I could shoot the wings off a fly back then."

Sharyn called county social services to come and check on him when she got outside. Despite his anger and his accusations, he was going to need help.

Was he right about his son-in-law? She drove straight to the office and was on the computer, looking for any information to substantiate his fears by the time the rest of the group arrived to start the day shift.

Cari stood beside her and chewed on one fingernail. "Weren't you happy with what I found about Walker?"

Sharyn continued to look at past domestic violence incident reports. "No, that was great. Thanks. This is stuff from last night." She told her about the apparent suicide.

"I could do that for you, Sheriff."

"You're scheduled to go out on patrol this morning."

"I was thinking that maybe I could stop going on patrol and just work here in the office. Would that be okay with you?"

Sharyn stopped what she was doing. "Cari, you have to get over this thing with Ernie. You can't work like this."

The other woman sighed. "I know. That's why I think I should turn in my resignation. That way you could find someone Ernie could work with."

"Not the way you handle a computer! Speaking of which, you're right. I'll have Joe go out with Ernie. Could you take a look at Vicky Rogers's computer? I need to make sure that the note came from there, and when it was written."

Cari smiled. "Thanks, Sheriff. I won't let you down."

"Don't thank me too much. Tomorrow, you go out on patrol. We're not going to talk about this again."

"But, Sheriff—"

"I have to get some coffee. I've been up all night, seen too much blood, and almost had my ear shot off. Thanks for taking over, Cari."

Nick and Ernie came in, looking as haggard as she felt. She glanced at her watch. Trudy was ten minutes late. Trudy was never late. Sharyn felt a sinking sensation in the pit of her stomach. What would she do without Trudy?

"I thought you were going home to get some rest." Ernie took off his hat and gun. He glanced at Cari but didn't speak to her.

Sharyn told him about Admiral Vendicott's accusations. "I came back and tried to find any mention of trouble between Mrs. Rogers and her husband. But so far, no domestic-violence issues or anything else. He didn't leave the mill after his shift started at three yesterday afternoon, according to his supervisor. I think he's clear. What did you find?"

Nick held up a plastic bag with a prescription bottle inside. "She was on Zoloft. This is a new prescription. I thought you might want her doctor's name to check it out with him. I'll take the bottle and see what I can get off of it. I've got the Beretta she was holding. We'll see if the bullet matches up. It looks pretty straightforward to me."

She agreed. "I don't really see anything suspicious about this, either. But after talking with the admiral, we have to follow through."

Both men groaned.

Nick patted his flat stomach. "Can we have breakfast first?"

"*We* can. But Ernie has patrol today with Joe."

Joe protested as he came down the stairs and heard their conversation. "I thought I was gonna get to work on the homicide. I thought Ernie and Cari were patrolling today."

The question hung in the basement between the sound of the phone ringing and an incoming fax.

Ernie glanced around the makeshift office. "Where's Trudy?"

Sharyn shook her head. "She's late."

"I should've hit Roy harder!" Ernie jammed his hat back on his head and pushed his gun into the holster with unnecessary force. "Come on, Joe. Let's go by the Bojangles so I can drown my sorrows with an egg biscuit."

Joe cleaned his sunglasses. "A biscuit isn't gonna do it. I need a dozen hot doughnuts from Krispy Kreme."

Nick cleared his throat as Ernie and Joe left. "I'll settle for some eggs and hash browns across the street, washed down with plenty of their bad coffee. Once you have a few cups of that stuff, you *can't* go to sleep."

Trudy's light laughter echoed from the stairway. She emerged in the basement with her hand tucked through Ed's arm. "Sorry I'm late, Sheriff. We went up to see the sunrise from Diamond Mountain. You forget how beautiful it is after you haven't been there for a while. Everything is so green up there now. It's like Mother Nature came down and blessed those poor burned-up hills."

Sharyn was amazed to see the light in Trudy's eyes and the big smile on her face. She hadn't seen her look so radiant since Ben died. She didn't say anything about her being late. "I'm glad you had such a good time. I'm on my way out. Ernie and Joe are on patrol. Cari is working here today. Ed, you're with me."

"Thanks, Sheriff." Trudy gave Ed a kiss before she all but floated to her desk.

Ed winked at her then left with Nick and Sharyn.

They were waiting to cross Main Street before Sharyn said anything. She wanted to make sure Trudy didn't hear her. "Ed, this better be the real thing for you."

He ran his hand through his blond curls. "I don't know what you mean, Sheriff."

"I mean this thing with you and Trudy. You'd better be planning on marrying her if you somehow manage to make her love you. If you break her heart, I'm going to kick your butt."

He glanced at Nick for backup. "Marriage? I'm forty-eight years old. I haven't ever been married because I know what a major mistake that would be. I'm not husband material."

Sharyn grabbed his shirtsleeve. "Then why have you been chasing her for so long? Why this sudden new glow between you?"

"Well, we don't want her going to work for Roy, do we?" His baby-blue eyes widened. "I'm stepping up to take care of that problem."

Morning traffic cleared briefly as the light changed. They ran across the street together. A car horn sounded anyway. People in Diamond Springs had become less tolerant as the town continued to grow.

Sharyn rounded on Ed, pushing her finger into his broad chest until he was against the brick wall beside the diner. "I can't *believe* you said that! Don't you have any feelings at all for her?"

Ed appealed to Nick. "Back me up here, buddy. Men are different. Some men get married. Some men don't. I'm one of the last ones. Nick understands, don't you?"

Nick laughed. "You've got to be kidding! I'm not jumping in here."

"I don't want you to romance Trudy so that she stays with the sheriff's department." Sharyn emphasized each word. "I'll tell her what you're up to before I see her hurt again."

Ed smiled. It was "the smile." It had won hundreds of hearts and gotten him out of some tough spots. "I wouldn't hurt Trudy for the world, you know that. I love her. In my way. I just don't wanna talk about getting married."

Sharyn knew she had to be satisfied with that. There wasn't much else she could do without telling Trudy. She started to walk away from Ed when he put his arms around her and hugged her. "What's that for?"

"Because you're so cute when you're all riled up. Kind of like a mama possum protecting her babies."

"You're crazy, Ed."

"Remember when you were little and you used to call me Uncle Ed? I remember taking you to the drive-in that Saturday night after Johnny Miller stood you up for the dance."

"I remember all of that. And I remember my dad talking about your girlfriends. And I'm telling you now that I can be as mean as a possum. If you dump Trudy for some young floozy, I'm going to show you my teeth."

"You don't have to worry. I'll take care of Trudy."

Nick sighed. "Can we eat now?"

"Sure." Sharyn turned away from Ed's million-dollar smile.

"So, that's the trick, huh?" Nick teased her as he opened the door to the diner. "We have an argument, and I smile a lot, and compare you to a marsupial. That's what I've been doing wrong all this time."

She laughed at him as he sat beside her in a booth. "Yeah. That's it. Next time we argue, try that."

Over breakfast, they discussed the information they had about Clint Walker. Cari couldn't find anything out of the ordinary about his life. He paid his taxes, sent his kids to private school, earned good money as an insurance salesman. He supported local charities, coached a kids' softball team, and was a member of the local Moose and Shriners' Lodges.

"Then eight years ago, he seems to have disappeared," Sharyn told them. "No more attendance at charity events mentioned in the paper. No more softball teams' winning games. The taxes were still paid on the house and life seemed to go on. Except for the personal property taxes, insurance and registration on a 1992 Mercedes."

"Interesting since the kids told me this morning that the car in the cemetery is a 1992 Mercedes." Nick buttered his toast.

"But why wouldn't somebody report that this pillar of the community was missing?" Ed smiled at the young waitress who walked by.

Sharyn kicked him in the shin. "That's a good question." She told him about her experience with Walker's wife. "I think we're going to have her come in." Her cell phone rang before she could say anything else. When she'd finished talking to Trudy, she said, "Well, I guess we don't have to do anything. Ladonna Walker is waiting for us at the office."

"With her high-priced lawyer?" Ed guessed.

"With Caison Talbot." She finished her coffee. "I already hate this week."

SIX

THERE WAS AN eight-by-ten room in the courthouse basement that Sharyn had converted into an interrogation/conference room. It wouldn't hold the big table from the old sheriff's office. Instead, they put a folding table in the middle of the room and set six folding chairs around it.

Sharyn ignored Caison using his handkerchief to clean off a seat for Mrs. Walker. She sat down with Ed and took out her file on the case. "I appreciate you coming in today, Mrs. Walker."

Ladonna looked at Caison. He nodded and she answered, "Of course, Sheriff."

"We have a few questions we'd like you to answer about your husband," Sharyn continued.

Ladonna looked at Caison. He nodded and she answered, "I'll try to answer your questions."

Ed sat back in his chair and Sharyn sighed. It was going to be a long interview.

"I'm sure you appreciate that my client is under tremendous stress, Sheriff," Caison interrupted her. "She's willing to cooperate in this matter but it's very difficult for her."

Sharyn smiled. "I'll try to make this as painless as

possible, sir. Mrs. Walker, do you know where your husband is?"

After getting permission from her lawyer, the woman replied, "Not exactly."

"Could you be more specific?"

"I haven't seen or spoken to my husband in about eight years."

Ed jumped in. "And you didn't report him missing?" He glanced at Sharyn. "Sorry."

"I didn't think to," Mrs. Walker replied. "He's been gone before without letting me know where he was. I suppose I thought he'd just come back one day. I didn't want to make a fuss and cause a lot of embarrassment."

Sharyn tapped her pen on the file folder. "Weren't you worried about him? I mean, even if he was gone for a few months before this, eight years is a long time."

Ladonna dabbed a lacy handkerchief at her heavily made-up eyes. Her glossy, dark red hair was teased up high around her chubby face. "Don't you think I've been worried, Sheriff? Don't you think I've gone to bed every night alone for the past eight years praying that Clint would at least call me? You don't know what it's been like raising little Clint and Donna alone without my husband!"

They all waited while she dissolved into tears, comforted by Caison. Ed rolled his eyes and got up to pace the room. Sharyn got the woman a glass of water. Trudy came into the room with an apologetic smile and gave Sharyn a fax.

When Ladonna was able to face them again, her face

looked like a worried raccoon. "I'm sorry, Sheriff. I don't know what's come over me. I can usually handle this. Well, I've *been* handling it for the past eight years. It's not like there haven't been questions before. I just tell everyone that he's out of town for a while."

Sharyn found it hard to believe that no one had looked any deeper into Walker's disappearance. But the proof seemed to be in the lack of a missing person's report filed by friends, Moose Lodge buddies, or co-workers. "I'm sorry, Mrs. Walker. I know this has to be difficult for you. I'm afraid I'm going to have to make it even harder. A few days ago, we found the body of a man buried in his car in the old Union Cemetery."

Ladonna nodded as she tried to wipe the mascara and eyeliner from her face. "I've heard about that, Sheriff. But why are you telling me now?"

"We just received more information on that discovery. The body of the man we found is unidentifiable right now. But he had a wallet in his back pocket with your husband's driver's license and Social Security card in it."

The woman gasped and dug bright red fingernails into the sleeve of Caison's imported Italian suit coat.

"We can't be completely sure but we think that it's your husband. The license and registration for the Mercedes we found matches your husband's car."

Large, fat tears rolled down Ladonna's face. "You mean Clint is dead? Why can't you identify him? Let me see him! I can tell you if it's him. I was married to the man for twenty years."

Sharyn tried to find a nice way to skirt that issue. "I'm afraid it's not that easy."

"What do you mean, Sheriff? I think I should know my own husband." She glanced at Caison for support. "I demand that you take me to see him."

"He's been dead for a long time," Ed told her. "He doesn't have a face."

Ladonna Walker fainted for the second time in her life. She fell sideways against Caison who couldn't move her from that position. Ed and Sharyn had to help him out from under her. Then the three of them laid her on the floor.

"Thanks, Ed." Sharyn dialed 9-1-1 and asked for the paramedics. "I could've said that. I was trying to avoid something like this happening again."

Caison was using his handkerchief to fan his client's face. "Well you weren't doing a very good job. Next time, I demand that you leave him out of my client's interviews."

Trudy showed the paramedics into the small room. Sharyn, Ed, and Caison had to leave for them to reach Mrs. Walker.

"Is everything you have circumstantial about this man in the car?" Caison asked Sharyn as the paramedics tried to revive his client. "You don't even know for sure if it is Clint."

"So far. But even circumstantial evidence can add up. We haven't been able to locate any medical records that Nick can use to verify the body's ID. There might be something Mrs. Walker can tell us that we can use.

Otherwise, we'll have to go to a DNA match with one of his children. You know how long that would take."

He nodded. "I'll talk to her. But I know what you're thinking. And let me tell you right now that this woman had nothing to do with her husband's disappearance."

"You know what I'm thinking because none of this makes any sense. No one would go so far to keep up with appearances while her husband vanishes off the face of the earth, unless she has something to hide."

"I want it duly noted that my client has been co-operative. She has nothing to hide and wants to find the truth as much as anyone else. Besides, what would her motive for murder be? Mr. Walker was the sole support of his family before he disappeared. My client had every reason to want her husband alive and well." His voice rose as he spoke, until he sounded like a preacher in the small basement.

No one looked up. They were all too familiar with Caison to pay any attention to his grandstanding. But Sharyn knew that wouldn't be the case once the press was involved. "I hope you're right. But I think it's good that she retained counsel. What happened to Mr. Walker wasn't an accident. Your client is probably at the top of our suspect list."

Caison shook her hand. "Thank you for being so candid. I'm sure you'll do what you have to do to get to the truth."

The lead paramedic walked out of the room. "She says she feels fine, Sheriff. She seems okay."

Sharyn thanked him then let Caison help Mrs.

Walker out of the building. He promised to be in touch. They both knew there wasn't enough evidence to hold the woman. Especially since the dead man might not even be her husband.

"Yeah, right," Ed remarked when they were gone. "I thought Talbot was only working on getting his son out of prison?"

"I guess he had to do something between appeals," Sharyn speculated. "But I think he'll convince her to help us find some way to ID the body. It's in her best interest."

"I don't know about that, Sheriff. She's guilty as all get out." Ed sat down at his desk. "I've heard some really good fake crying in my life and that wasn't it. Why would she want to help us?"

"Does she strike you as the kind of woman who would shoot a man then bury him in his car? I can't see her running the piece of equipment it would take to do that. For that matter, a gun seems a little messy."

"She seems more like the poison type to me," Cari added.

"And Caison's right, much as it pains me to admit it," Sharyn continued. "What did she gain from his death? Because she refused to tell anyone he was gone, she couldn't even collect on his insurance. He still has a large life insurance policy with her as beneficiary. It seems to me it was more trouble to raise her children alone and sit around waiting for him to come home. My mother knew them. Apparently, Mr. Walker was quite the ladies' man."

Ed laughed. "You'd never guess it to look at him."

"Don't get started. We have a lot to do today. We're going to see the Walkers' children and pay a visit to a few of Clint's friends. Then we're going to see Vicky Rogers's doctor."

Cari took some sheets of paper, put them into a green file folder and gave them to Sharyn. "Here's what I have for you so far."

CLINT WALKER JUNIOR worked at the First Federal bank in downtown Diamond Springs. The branch manager was good enough to let them use the bank's conference room to talk.

"Are you saying that my father's dead?" Clint was a good-looking young man in a somber, rather serious way. His brown suit was conservative like his haircut. He was medium height, medium build, no tattoos or pierced ears. He had very direct blue eyes and was very well spoken. Not the charmer Sharyn imagined his father had been.

"He might be, son," Ed replied in a quiet tone.

Clint Junior seemed lost for words. He glanced around the room and adjusted his tie. "I guess I always expected something like this. He's been gone since I was fourteen. No letters. No phone calls. My mother wouldn't talk about it. I think she believed he ran away with another woman."

Sharyn picked up on that. "Did she talk to you about him being unfaithful?"

"No! Never. But Donna and I both remember them

arguing about it. There was one woman in particular. I'm sorry. I don't remember her name. But Donna and I lay in bed together one night for hours while they were fighting. We both thought that was the end. But the next morning, everything was back to normal. Maybe he gave her up. I don't know."

"I understand. And I'm sorry I don't have better news for you." Sharyn put away her notebook. "I'll let you know as soon as the investigation is complete. Right now, there's still the chance that this man we found isn't your father. But we have to investigate."

"I realize that." Clint Junior smiled. "You know, I always had this fantasy about him coming back. He'd been in an accident and had amnesia all these years. But as soon as he remembered who he was, he came back to us. I guess that isn't going to happen."

She gave him her card. "If you have any questions or you think of anything else that might help us, please give me a call."

"I will. Thanks, Sheriff. You should talk to my sister. She was older. She might remember more. She owns a little boutique on Eighth Street."

Sharyn shook his hand. "We'll do that. Thanks."

DONNA WALKER'S HAT BOUTIQUE was a few doors down from where the new sheriff's department was going up. Nothing was left of the old Clement's Building except for a bronze plaque in a small garden area. It acted as a memorial for the people who'd lost their lives in the fire that destroyed the building.

Ed and Sharyn parked on the street and walked around the corner past the site. The foundation for the new office was in place. A sign near the construction showed a picture of what the building would look like when it was finished.

"Two years." Ed watched the construction workers. "It's going to be a long time in that basement."

"Yeah. But at least they didn't decide to move us out into the county." Sharyn stood with her hands on the fence that separated the sidewalk from the construction.

He studied her for a moment. "Doesn't it bother you? I mean, everybody must be thinking that Roy is king. He's gonna be sitting in your daddy's old office."

"It bothers me more than we're never going to get along. He holds such a grudge against Dad. He'll never let me forget that."

"Don't forget *you* beat his butt in two elections." Ed laughed as they began walking again. "I think it might bother him more that he wouldn't be anybody, except that he was handy when the commission decided to create the new police force."

She smiled and pushed her hat back a little on her head. "There is that."

It was already almost ninety degrees outside when they walked into the boutique. The air-conditioning felt good. It was only May. They were in for a hot summer. Not hot and dry like the past two summers. This one appeared to be as wet as those were dry.

Donna Walker looked a lot like her mother. She was smaller and wore her dark red hair back in a

net-covered braid. Her clothes were as somber as her
brother's. But there the similarity ended. "Hello, Sheriff. Are you here to ask for a blood sample? Or can we
just do that swab in the mouth like they do on TV?"

Sharyn took off her hat and ruffled her damp hair
with her fingers. "I'm afraid I'm not as exciting as the
crime scene people. All I have is a pen and a notebook.
No swabs or needles."

Donna laughed. "I love your hat! Mind if I try it on?"

"It's a little sweaty," Sharyn started, but it was too
late. The heavy tan hat was swept from her fingers and
placed on Donna's head.

"It's a little big on me," she said. "Try one of mine.
I know you can't wear anything else on the job. But
you must wear other things when you're not working.
I read in Debbie Siler's gossip column that you're dating that hot medical examiner. He can come and swab
my mouth anytime!"

"Got anything for men?" Ed moved towards her with
his most charming smile plastered on his tan face.

Sharyn put her booted foot in his way. He nearly tripped
over it and gave her a killing look. "I'm afraid we're here
to discuss something more serious, Ms. Walker."

"I know." She gave the hat back. "My mother called
me this morning. And my brother called me about five
minutes ago. So, the prodigal father returns?"

Sharyn was surprised by her attitude. "I don't think
you understand. We believe your father may have been
murdered."

Donna sat down on a stool near one of the hat racks

and crossed her long legs. "And I'm supposed to be devastated? The only thing that bothers me about it is that my mother can't collect child support from a dead man. He left us. She wouldn't admit it. Probably went to live with his girlfriend over in Indian Creek. I think she was having his baby."

"Do you know her name?" Sharyn asked her.

"Barbara or Betty. Something like that. I never saw her but she was the only one my father was ever serious about. The other ones didn't mean anything, I guess. They were just fun to be with. He wouldn't have left my mother for them."

"But you think it's possible he was living with this woman in Indian Creek?"

"I know they were living together. I know she was pretty young. I remember that from their arguments. I went with my mother to look for her. Mom was going to beg her to leave my father alone. Can you imagine?"

"Do you think your mother knows her name?"

Donna shook her head. "I'm not sure. You'll have to ask her."

Sharyn put her pen into her pocket. "Is there anything you can think of that might help us identify your father's body? We don't have conclusive ID. We can do DNA from you or your brother but it will take a while."

The young woman considered the request. "I can't think of anything right now. My mother would probably know more than me."

Ed gave her his card. "If you think of anything, be

sure to give me a call *personally*." His fingers slid down hers as he left the card in her hand.

Sharyn sighed. Her mother always said you couldn't change a leopard's spots. She was probably talking about Ed. But if Trudy could live with it, knowing how he was, it wasn't any of her business. "Thanks for your time, Ms. Walker. Call us if you have any questions. I'll let you know what we find out."

Donna's eyes were riveted on Ed. "I'll be *sure* to call."

Sharyn nudged him when they got outside. "What was *that* all about?"

"I don't know what you mean, Sheriff. I was helping you question the family member."

"Oh, Ed. I wish you and Trudy would get married and go travel somewhere in a Winnebago."

He put one arm around her shoulders and hugged her. "No you don't. You wouldn't know what to do without me. Now, what about that doctor we're going to see? I think his office comes before the Moose Lodge."

She glanced at her notes as they got into the Jeep. "You're right, for once. Except there's no point in going to the Lodge. They only meet there once a month. We're going out to see John Schmidt. He's the head Moose or whatever. I'm hoping he might help complete the picture we're starting to get on Mr. Walker."

"Sounds good to me. What about lunch? Is there food in the plan somewhere?"

"We'll see if there's time."

He frowned. "I don't like working with you. Joe's

too serious for me but at least he eats a few times a day. You're gonna starve yourself down to nothing if you're not careful."

"I don't think I have to worry about that. You're just lucky you don't have to work with Ernie today."

"Yeah, I suppose so." He rolled his eyes as he fastened his seat belt. "And you should know. Marvella told me Ernie moved in with you. How's Nick taking it?"

She pulled out of the parking space and headed for the Dotger Clinic. "Don't go there, Ed. Or you won't be eating lunch all week."

DOCTOR WILLIAM MACEY was busy with patients when they arrived at the clinic. He managed to squeeze them in for a few minutes. He refused to discuss particulars about Vicky Rogers but agreed that he was treating her for depression. He did say that her depression wasn't serious and that he didn't feel that she was suicidal. But he'd only been treating her for a short time and a specific problem. When Sharyn tried to push him for any other answers, he gave her a card and told her to speak to his attorney.

"That wasn't much," Ed summed up when they got back in the Jeep. "Now what?"

Sharyn wasn't sure. "The admiral was very certain about Vicky not committing suicide. She *was* being treated for depression, but her doctor doesn't think she was suicidal. The admiral thinks her husband killed her but Stan's got an alibi for that night and there was no history of domestic violence. I guess we need to talk to some of her friends, besides Mrs. Marshal."

She stopped at a drive-through burger shack and called Ernie while Ed got his lunch. There was still a slim chance that the admiral was right about his daughter. But if nothing showed up with her friends or co-workers, she was going to have to call it what it seemed. Even with Dr. Macey's assurance that Vicky *probably* wasn't suicidal, the evidence seemed to contradict him. Sharyn realized that he might be worried about his malpractice insurance. After all, one of his patients who *shouldn't* have committed suicide was dead. And the admiral, like most people, had more trouble accepting that someone they loved committed suicide than if they were murdered.

It was almost two in the afternoon when they got to John Schmidt's house in one of the new subdivisions going up around Diamond Springs. John was the head of the county building inspectors. He'd helped the sheriff's department on a few cases. When a gang of thieves vandalized his son's house across the street last year, John let them set up surveillance in his home.

"Hello, Sheriff." John's wife, Mary Jo, met them at the front door. "Hi, Ed. Come on inside and have some tea. It's hotter than you-know-where out there. I can't believe it's only May."

"Thanks." Sharyn lowered her voice. "How's he holding up?"

Mary Jo shrugged. "He'll live. Just can't stand doing nothing. I told him if he doesn't want to get hurt, he should be more careful. Imagine a man his age climbing out on a half-finished roof!"

Ed was affronted by her words. "You women don't understand. It's not just a job, it's who we are. Where's John? He needs male sympathy."

"He's through there, in the sunroom. I'll get that tea while you talk."

Mary Jo and John were two of everyone's favorite people in Diamond Springs. They were similar in height and build; both a little round and short. They'd been married almost forty years, yet hardly anyone knew of them spending time apart unless John was working. Mary Jo was active in charity work and helping take care of her twin grandbabies who lived with her son.

"Thank goodness!" John switched off the TV with the remote. "Even with this new cable, there's nothing on during the day."

Ed whistled in admiration when he saw John's upper body cast. "You look like you fell off a roof, buddy. You'd better learn how to bounce if you're gonna do stuff like that."

John brought his hand to his chest. "Don't make me laugh. It hurts when I laugh."

Sharyn sat on the sofa opposite him. "Well, we have something pretty serious to ask you about, so it shouldn't hurt too much." She told him about the car in the cemetery and their investigation.

"You know, we've talked about Clint at almost every meeting for the last eight years." John grimaced as he repositioned himself in the recliner.

"Didn't anyone think about calling to report him as missing?" She pushed the table with his medication closer so he could reach it.

"Thanks, Sharyn. Ladonna kept telling us he was out of town. It's not that we didn't ask her. But you know groups. As fine an organization as the Moose Lodge is, even longtime members drift away. We kind of thought she was putting us off. I guess we never thought to question it."

"I'm having some trouble believing a person could go missing for eight years and no one thought to question it. We live in a small town. People know where I live, when I'm out at night, and who I'm with. Yet this man, fairly well-known in the community, vanishes, and everyone just thinks he's constantly out of town."

Mary Jo joined them in the cheerful sunroom with a trayful of glasses and a pitcher of iced tea. "Oh, goody! Are we gossiping about someone in town?"

Ed stood up to help her with the tray. "Clint Walker. He was a member of the Lodge with John. Maybe you know his wife, Ladonna?"

The smile faded from Mary Jo's animated face. She would've dropped the tray but Ed's hands were already on it. "Excuse me. I forgot something in the kitchen."

They waited until she left then Sharyn turned to John. "What's wrong with Mary Jo?"

John took a glass from Ed. "Thanks. It's like you say, Sharyn. It *is* a small town. And everybody knows everybody else's business. I'm afraid Mary Jo doesn't think too highly of Clint. Ladonna is her cousin's niece.

Everybody knows how he treated her. Telling her he was going out of town when he was down at The Bridge Motel with some tramp. Always tight-fisted with the money so the kids had to do without."

Sharyn nodded. "We haven't heard many good things about Mr. Walker. Do you think that's why no one reported him missing?"

"That, and he was always lying. He'd tell Ladonna he was playing golf with me or going hunting with Eldeon. He even told her he was at the Lodge when he was really fooling around. A man like that, no one really misses him. It's probably been a blessing to her that he was gone. She just tried to save face all these years."

Ed had an unusually sober look on his face. "My mama taught me that it wasn't right to speak ill of the dead. Just because a man gets around doesn't make him a bad person. I can't believe nobody cared about what happened to him."

"You're right, I expect." John took his medication. "I wish I could tell you more. We weren't close. It's hard to get close to a man like that. Are you sure that's him in the car?"

"Not yet," Sharyn admitted. "But I think we will be soon. Thanks for your help."

"You're not leaving already, are you? You're the best thing that's happened to me all week."

Ed was ready to go, too. "Maybe I'll come by and we can watch Duke clobber Tennessee Saturday."

John shook his finger at him. "You wish! But if you come, I'll provide the snacks."

Sharyn left them planning for the game and went to find Mary Jo. The other woman was in the kitchen. Water was running full force down the drain while she stared out the window. "Are you okay?"

Mary Jo shook herself and turned off the water. She wrapped a towel around her hand. "Fool me—I burned myself making the tea. I guess I'm just getting old."

"I'm learning to cook. Anytime I can do it and *not* burn myself, it's a miracle." She studied Mary Jo's blotchy face. She looked like she'd been crying. "Would you like me to take a look at it?"

"No, I'm fine. I've got a jar of those ginger pickles your Aunt Selma loves so much. I called her last week, but I guess she's too busy with her new beau to come get them. Maybe you could take them out to her. There's a jar for you, too."

Sharyn thanked her and took the jars of pickles. She joined Ed outside and stowed the jars in the backseat. "That was strange."

"You mean Mary Jo? You know she's like that with everyone. She's got a soft heart. John told me once that she cries even when the movie ends good."

She started the Jeep. "You're probably right. Let's get back to town and see what else has come up."

TRUDY MET THEM at the foot of the basement stairs. She handed Sharyn her messages then kissed Ed. He reciprocated with even more enthusiasm than usual.

Sharyn ignored them and went to her desk. Ernie and Joe followed them into the building. She knew

Marvella and JP would be in soon. It was time to put all of the information together. She tried to call Nick but only reached his voice mail. He'd called and faxed her while she was gone.

It was a tight squeeze but they all managed to get into the makeshift conference room. Ed and Ernie stood against the wall so that Trudy could be in there with them.

"We talked to a few people Mrs. Rogers worked with before she moved out to Claraville," Ernie began explaining. "All of them were shocked at the idea of her being depressed or suicidal. They all described her as a very happy person."

"But they all agreed that she didn't want to move to Claraville. She felt like she had to, so she could help her father," Joe continued. "She quit her job about six months ago because it took too long to drive into town."

"And none of them knew anything about problems between her and Mr. Rogers," Ernie added. "But those could've started in the past six months. A couple can be really close but have problems come up that they can't deal with."

Ed interrupted before Ernie became maudlin. He told them what Dr. Macey had said, as little as that was. "Sounds to me like the woman just went off the deep end. She wasn't happy living out of town. She didn't want to give up her job. It's a terrible thing but it happens. I think this is shaping up to be a suicide."

Trudy held out a stack of pink memo notes. "The admiral disagrees. A lot."

Sharyn sat back in her chair. "What about the note, Cari?"

"It was typed on her computer about the same time Nick says she died. I took the keyboard over to him this afternoon. The only fingerprints showing up on it belong to Vicky Rogers." Cari glanced at Ed. "I think I have to agree with you."

"We know no one wants their daughter to be a suicide," Sharyn confirmed. "But I think we've covered all the angles here. I don't think there's anywhere else to go."

"Think again." Nick stood in the doorway behind her. "I have a little surprise in store for you."

SEVEN

Ernie groaned. "I hate it when he says that, even worse than I hate the Sheriff's gut feelings. They both mean trouble."

Nick got a chair and sat in the doorway since there wasn't room for him anywhere around the table. "You know, we could have these discussions over at the morgue. I think I have a closet bigger than this one."

There was general discontent with his words. Joe wadded up a piece of paper and threw it at him. Marvella prayed for strength.

"If you're done giving me a hard time, I have some information that you need." Nick took some papers from his briefcase then set the case on the floor under his feet. "I don't have any startling revelation about Vicky Rogers as far as whether or not she committed suicide. But I found something unusual."

"Nick, you should've been an actor," Ed told him with a smile. "You love to make it dramatic."

Cari giggled and Trudy glanced at her sharply.

"Everyone settle down." Sharyn scooted her chair to one side so she could see Nick. "Let's hear what he has to say."

"On the Rogers's case—the bullet I removed from

Vicky Rogers was from a Beretta 92, 9 mm semiautomatic. Probably made in the late seventies. Nice pistol." Nick put on his black-rimmed glasses and glanced at his notes. "This particular weapon happens to be registered to Admiral George Vendicott. But that's not what makes it interesting."

"We're not gonna be out on patrol until midnight at this rate," Marvella grumbled, glancing at her watch.

Nick continued reading, ignoring her. "Mrs. Rogers had GSR on her hand that was holding the weapon as well as on her face. I believe she was holding the pistol to her head when it was fired. I'm not saying if she had help or not. There's nothing forensic that confirms or denies that possibility. But the husband and the friend were clean. The rest of that is up to you people. Best guess, I'd say it was a suicide. She'd taken a lot of Valium a couple of hours before she died. But that fits in with the time she wrote the note, according to Cari, and it's not unusual."

"Anything to make sure you get the job done," Ernie suggested.

"The dose wasn't lethal. It was enough that she'd be groggy but that's about it. Most people take the whole bottle to be sure. Either that was all she had or she thought it was enough. I went back to her house and there was no sign of her having any drugs besides the Zoloft. Not even an empty bottle where she got the Valium from. I called her doctor but he didn't issue a prescription for it. But I checked at the same time and the admiral has a prescription for Valium." He looked up from his notes. "Of course, I know a dozen people who take Valium and they regularly offer it to me. No one seems to understand what a prescription means anymore."

Everyone thought about what he was saying. It was silent except for the sound of pens scratching on paper and the phone ringing in the other room.

"Now for the *really* interesting part." He rubbed his hands together and grinned. "This is what makes it all worthwhile. One of the bullets I took from the dead man in the Mercedes was from a Beretta 9 mm semi-automatic. Just on a whim, I tested and compared the two bullets—one from John Doe/Clint Walker and one from Vicky Rogers. They match."

Marvella sucked in her breath. "What does that mean?"

JP rubbed his chin thoughtfully. "The admiral shot Mr. Walker. Then his daughter borrowed the Beretta and his Valium to kill herself."

Sharyn interrupted his theory. "It doesn't mean anything yet. And if I read one scrap of this information in the *Gazette* tomorrow, I'm going to fire all of you. Just because the gun *belonged* to the admiral doesn't mean he was responsible for either shooting. Vicky was an adult. She took care of him. Presumably, she had access to the weapon and the drugs."

Marvella *tsked* and shook her head. "But what about Mr. Walker? I don't think he shot himself with the admiral's gun, Sheriff!"

Sharyn quickly rerouted the conversation. "Let me

remind everyone that this is a fact-finding investigation. We aren't ready to draw any conclusions yet. I don't want to hear any accusations until we're ready to make an arrest."

"Sorry, Sheriff." Marvella twisted the rose-covered scarf tied around her head. "I guess I just got carried away."

"You can't exactly look the other way here, either," Ernie suggested to Sharyn. "We may not know what the link is yet, but there's definitely a link. Two people were shot with the same gun, even if it was eight years apart."

"Before we commit to *anything*," Sharyn added, "let's get the facts straight. We need to find out if there was any other link between the admiral and Clint Walker."

"You said *one* of the bullets." Joe read back from his notes. "Was the other one different, Nick?"

"I think it was from another gun," Nick told him. "My assistants are checking it out right now. I have to let them do some of the research or they won't learn. I'll let you know when they have something on it."

"If that one links back to Admiral Vendicott, too," Ed considered, "that might be enough to have a serious conversation with the man."

"Especially if we find out that they had some common denominators," Cari finished with a flourish.

Nick wasn't finished. "I had a phone call late this afternoon. It was Caison Talbot. He said that he's representing the Walker family. Apparently Mrs. Walker remembered a motorcycle accident that Mr. Walker was involved in when he was a teenager. He had a small

sliver of metal left in his shin that he didn't have removed. It set off metal detectors when they traveled. I
haven't had a chance to check it out yet. But this could
be our breakthrough on substantiating that our John
Doe *is* Clint Walker."

Sharyn thanked Nick for his work then turned to
her deputies. "We'll start again tomorrow. Cari, you're
on patrol with Joe. Ernie, I need you on the computer."

"And that leaves me not getting enough to eat because I'm working with the sheriff," Ed mourned.
"Can't I go out with Cari and Joe?"

Sharyn didn't answer him. As far as she was concerned, he already knew what she was going to say.
"Any questions?"

"Yeah." Marvella raised her hand. "When do I get
to help out with the murder investigation?"

"I need you on the nightshift since we're short one
man," Sharyn explained. "If you'd like to work a double, you can help out. I'm sure we could use an extra
hand and it's good training. I just can't spare you or JP
from working at night."

"Maybe somebody would like to trade me shifts for
one day?" Marvella looked around the room but didn't
see any volunteers.

"We'll see what we can do," Ernie promised. "If
we're finished here, I think JP and you should be leaving on patrol."

"That's it." Sharyn ended the meeting and gathered
her notes. "Keep your ears open. There might be some
information out there that can help us."

Nick moved his chair out of the doorway so that

everyone could leave. He waited in the office for Sharyn while she talked to Cari and Trudy.

Ernie took Marvella's arm. "You're taking the scarf off, right?"

"It's not around my neck," she argued. "And with my hat on, you can barely see it."

He struck a pose. "Except for the *tiniest* splash of color against your collar. Just a hint of red and yellow roses."

She brightened. "Exactly!"

"Take it off."

"Boogerman!" Marvella ripped the scarf out of her black curls.

Ernie frowned. "What did you say?"

"I called you the Boogerman 'cause you go around trying to scare everyone."

"I know the sheriff likes you, Marvella. But she trusts me in these matters. Don't make me keep telling you about this stuff or I'll suspend you."

She saluted him but didn't say anything else.

Trudy turned on the automated switchboard before she left with Ed. ADA Toby Fisher showed up to take Cari out for dinner. Joe went home to his wife. Ernie sat down at his desk and started on some paperwork.

"Ready?" Nick asked Sharyn.

She glanced at Ernie. "We can't just leave him here alone."

"Why not? He's working. I was thinking about a nice, relaxing, quiet dinner for two at Fuigi's."

"I have to ask him. Then if he wants to stay anyway…"

"We can all work and order takeout?"

She shrugged then went to Ernie's desk. "Let's get some supper, huh?"

He looked at Nick. "I'm just going to stay here and catch up on some stuff. You two go ahead. I'll see you later."

Nick was happy with that. He started for the stairs. "See you later, Ernie."

But Sharyn wasn't satisfied. "It's not a big deal. We want you to come with us."

"Really? Are you sure?"

INSTEAD OF THE ROMANTIC Italian restaurant, they ended up at a noisy pizza place down by the lake. It was crowded with the members of a local basketball team celebrating their latest victory.

"This is good." Ernie munched some pizza as he sat between Nick and Sharyn.

"Yeah. Great." Nick drank some beer and pretended he was home asleep in front of his television.

Sharyn was beginning to get a headache. "I wonder if we could get them to turn down the music?"

Ernie leaned closer to her. "What?"

They didn't stay long once they'd finished eating. Nick had driven over with them from the office but decided to walk home from the Pizza Palace. His apartment was only a block away.

"Are you sure?" Sharyn stood outside and talked to him.

"I figure you and Ernie need some quality time alone. Just because you work in the same office and live together doesn't mean he shouldn't take up all of my time with you, too."

She kissed his chin. "You're so understanding."

"Not *that* understanding." He took her in his arms and kissed her for a long time. "Good night, Sharyn. I'll see you tomorrow."

She sighed as she let him go. "Good night."

"I'm messing with your whole life." Ernie watched Nick disappear up the sidewalk. "I wouldn't blame him if he shot me with all of his guns."

She turned the Jeep towards home. "I'm too tired to be any company tonight anyway. He has to feel the same."

Ernie complained and apologized all the way back to the apartment. Sharyn opened the downstairs door and locked it again behind them. There were two messages on her answering machine. The first one was from her sister, Kristie. She was coming down for Memorial Day weekend and wanted to have a strategy session about what she should be looking for in Jack Winter's office. She'd been working for him in Raleigh since she went back to college.

Sharyn erased the message and thought of all the things she planned to say to her sister. Kristie was naive to think that Jack didn't know she'd taken a job with his office to spy on him. All she was going to do was end up getting hurt.

The second message was from Jill Madison-Farmer. It was short and cryptic. She was meeting with a district court judge who might be willing to hear their petition

on behalf of Skeeter Johnson. She promised to get back
with Sharyn as soon as she had more information.

"Anything interesting?" Ernie asked when he came
in.

"Not really." She yawned. "I'm going to bed before
I fall down. See you tomorrow."

Sharyn went into her bedroom and locked the door.
She forced herself to shower and change before she took
out the little black book she'd found in her office. Sitting in the middle of her bed, she took out a notebook
to begin work on it. Her hands trembled as she opened
the book and glanced through it.

It was definitely her father's handwriting. She didn't
need an expert to tell her that. She realized that she
might need one to help her figure out what was written in the book. It was only forty pages long but every
page was crammed full of numbers and jumbled letters
that didn't make any sense.

She'd read a few things online about breaking codes.
People substituted a letter or number for each real letter and repeated the process. But where to start? The
information she'd read suggested starting with something simple that might be expected to be in the code.

Sharyn tried looking for JACK in each group of four
letters and numbers, but she couldn't find any that repeated themselves in the same way. She tried CAISON
in the groups of six letters and numbers, but it was still
no good.

Think smaller. She searched through the groups looking for letters that she could replace throughout the

book, starting with vowels. For each 7, she put A. But that didn't make any sense. She tried the same technique with all of the primary numbers but nothing she tried created words that meant anything. It was all gibberish.

She lay back on the bed a little after midnight and listened to the church bell tolling the hour. Her father wasn't a secretive man. Whatever he was hiding in this book was important. He had to be afraid that it would fall into the wrong hands to go to such elaborate methods to disguise it.

"What were you thinking when you did this?" she murmured, holding the book in her hand as she closed her eyes. "And how am I going to figure it out?"

She couldn't do anything more on it tonight. Her brain felt like mush. Worried that someone might find it, she tucked the book under her pillow and shut off her tiny reading light. She was just going to have to be patient. It might take time to decode it, but intuition told her that it was important and worth the effort.

ERNIE WAS ALREADY GONE the next morning when she got up. His sleeping bag was rolled up and stashed behind the bed in the spare room. That, and his satchel in the closet, were the only signs that he'd even been there last night. She smiled at his love of order. When he and Annie finally got together, he was going to make a terrific husband!

When she was dressed and ready to go, Sharyn put the codebook back into a small space she'd found behind her bathroom medicine cabinet. Despite being up late again, she felt rested and ready to work. The noose was tightening around Jack's throat and he didn't even know it. At least, she *hoped* he didn't know it.

Ernie met her at the office with a cup of coffee and a load of information. He'd been there since four. "The only substantial link I can find between the admiral and Walker is that they were both members of the Diamond Springs VFW. I found some photos from a picnic ten years ago that were published in the *Gazette*. There was a big group in Memorial Park that day. Both men were there with their wives."

"Good work!" She took a look at his information. "Do you think they knew each other in service?"

"I doubt it. The admiral served in World War II and Vietnam. Walker served briefly in Vietnam. But they were posted in different parts of that country. The admiral was in the Navy and Walker was in the Army."

"If Walker was in the military, I wonder why Nick can't find his prints."

"Some kind of backup with the FBI database," he replied. "I talked to him this morning. He might have more luck now that we know that Walker was in the Army."

"If they were both in the VFW, maybe we can check with someone else in the group and see if they remember any interaction between them. Where's Joe? Isn't he a member?"

"Nope. He wasn't interested." Ernie grinned. "Not enough action for him. Anyway, I sent him out to Claraville with Ed and Cari to settle an argument between two neighbors about a fence."

"Really? That seems like quite a few deputies to settle an argument."

"We're talking Hatfields and McCoys. We may have to join them if it gets any worse. There are at least twenty gun-toting family members holding each other off. It's not a pretty picture."

She raised one eyebrow. "Are you sure *we* shouldn't be out there, too?"

"Not yet. I thought we'd see if they can handle it. So what's on your agenda for today?"

"I guess finding someone from the VFW to talk to." She sipped her coffee.

He smiled his crooked Ernie smile. "One step ahead of you, as always. Guess who's been an active member of the VFW for thirty years?"

"Besides you?" she guessed. "Eldeon Percy."

"You're sharp as a tack this morning, aren't you? We have an appointment upstairs in a few minutes."

"What about you, Ernie?" Sharyn ignored the box of doughnuts on the table near the coffeepot. "Did you ever notice anything going on between the admiral and Mr. Walker?"

He ran his hand across his face. "I'm ashamed to say I haven't been that involved. I didn't even know they were members. I couldn't name you more than a few other vets that I know around here. Let's hope Mr. Percy paid more attention."

District Attorney Eldeon Percy was a tall, slender

man in his early sixties. His trademark white linen suits and languid manner in the courtroom marked him as a Southern gentleman. But everyone knew he was like a sleeping tiger. He might close his eyes and rest his head against his folded hands while he was listening, but he was only waiting to spring when his prey was finished speaking.

Sharyn had come up against him many times in court when he was a defense attorney. Usually, he managed to get his client acquitted. When Jack Winter decided to run for the North Carolina State senate, he appointed Mr. Percy to be District Attorney for the rest of his term. Now Percy was supposed to be on *her* side. Sometimes, she wasn't sure she could tell the difference. But at least she knew what to expect from a tiger, even an elegant, refined one. Winter was more like a snake. He never did what she expected him to do.

"Good morning, Sheriff. Deputy. Would you like some coffee?" Percy's assistant waited in the doorway until they told him they were fine. Then the young man closed the double doors behind him as he left the room.

"Good morning, sir. We appreciate you taking the time to talk to us." Ernie shook the DA's hand.

Sharyn always expected Mr. Percy to wipe his hand on his faultless white suit after he touched someone. She never saw it happen, but it was the impression she had of him. "We only have a few questions, Mr. Percy. They involve Admiral Vendicott."

He nodded. "George. A fine man. A fine officer."

"Yes, sir. Did you know Captain Clint Walker?"

Ernie sat down in one of the chairs near the front of the neat desk.

Percy closed his eyes and clasped his hands together. "I don't believe I recognize that name, Deputy."

Sharyn gave him a photocopy of a picture they had of Walker. "This is from ten years ago. He's been missing for the past eight years. His wife is named Ladonna. They have two children and live on the same side of Diamond Mountain Lake as you do."

Startling blue eyes opened and focused on her face. "A very good description, Sheriff." He glanced at the photocopy. "Yes. I do faintly remember him. Skirt chaser, right?"

Ernie smiled. "From what we've been told."

"Yes. He wasn't very active in the group. He was more interested in the female officers and the wives of the male officers. He even went so far as to make advances at my daughter, Selena. I can tell you that she put him back in his place *very* quickly. He wasn't a man we needed in the group. Good thing he wasn't more active. If he would've been, we'd probably have thrown him out. Why do you ask?"

This seemed to be the story of Clint Walker's life. Men hated him and women loved him. Sharyn was glad that she'd never met him. She explained about finding the body in the Mercedes, even though she knew Percy kept up with what went on in town. He could probably tell *her* a thing or two about things that happened. "What about the admiral's family, sir? Did Mr. Walker make advances at his wife or daughter?"

JOYCE & JIM LAVENE

"I don't really know, Sheriff. That's a rather personal matter. If he came in contact with them, I feel sure he did. He was that kind of man." Percy leaned back in his chair. "What is it that you're looking for here? What do you think George did? I hope you're not suggesting he was involved in any way with Captain Walker."

"I'm not really sure if he's done anything. We're just tracking down a lead. Mr. Walker was shot by the same gun that Vicky Rogers used to commit suicide. That gun is registered to the admiral."

"And that has led you to believe that George is somehow responsible for shooting Captain Walker eight years ago?"

"It *does* make sense, sir. We believe Mrs. Rogers borrowed the gun from her father. She probably didn't know it was involved in the other shooting. We wouldn't know either except for her death. But that puts the admiral right in the middle of our investigation into Mr. Walker's death."

He got to his feet in one lithe movement. "Then I suggest you get out there and do some better investigation, Sheriff. George has been in contact with me. He seems to feel that his daughter's death wasn't a suicide. Are you aware of *that* concern?"

Sharyn refused to back down from him. "Yes, sir. But there's no evidence to substantiate that theory. No parent wants to think their child could kill herself."

"As I said, I hold him in the greatest esteem," he reiterated for her benefit. "There had better be some irrefutable evidence for me to seek an arrest warrant for him on this Walker case. Just because a gun is registered to someone doesn't mean that person used it. I'm sure you're aware of that, Sheriff."

Sharyn hated the way he always managed to make her feel like she was still a freshman in high school. "We'll find the truth, Mr. Percy. That's what we do. I hope it doesn't involve the admiral. But if it does, I'll expect your cooperation." She shook his cold hand, then walked out the door with Ernie.

"That was some tough talk," Ernie remarked when they were on their way back to the office. "Do you think the admiral shot Clint Walker?"

"At this point, it's a pretty good bet. Maybe Walker got a little too frisky with his wife. The admiral has a notorious temper. Someone else *could* have used the Beretta, but what are the chances that it wasn't its owner?"

"That would at least give him some motive. And what are the chances Walker wasn't killed by an angry husband?" Ernie questioned. "But from what we've heard, the admiral would have to stand in line to want to kill him. But the way Mr. Percy sounded, you're going to have to prove none of the other would-be killers got there first."

"Which, given the fact that he was killed so long ago that no one will be able to prove where they were or what they were doing, should be interesting." She took the keys to the Jeep out of her pocket. "I think we should pay the admiral another visit. Maybe he can say something to clarify this for us."

Ernie's nose twitched. "And if he doesn't have an

alibi for whatever night and time it was that Walker was killed?"

"Then we're exactly where we are right now. Ready?"

BUT THEY WEREN'T able to see Admiral Vendicott again that day. He'd suffered another stroke during the night and been hospitalized in critical condition. His doctor told them that he might not be able to answer any questions even if he regained consciousness. This stroke had been even more severe than his first one. There was probably brain damage.

Ernie and Sharyn looked in on him through the ICU window. The old man looked dead already, his parchment-white skin barely covering his bones.

"He's not breathing on his own," the doctor explained. "Someone in the family might have to make a decision on whether or not to leave him on the machine. There's no Living Will that we could find. Do you know if he has any next of kin around here now that his daughter is gone?"

"He told me he was alone," Sharyn answered. "What happens in cases like that?"

He sighed and adjusted his glasses. "The board of trustees for the hospital makes the decision. We'll see how things go. He could pull out of it enough to be transferred to a nursing home. It would be their problem then."

Ernie shivered and walked away. Sharyn thanked the doctor for his time and they went down in the elevator together.

"Sorry state when you get old, Sheriff."

"Yeah, I know."

He took a deep breath and got back to the business at hand. "Well, that covers the whole thing up nice and neat. The admiral dies and takes the answers with him."

"That doesn't work for me. There has to be another way to find out what happened to Walker. It's just as bad to be forgotten because no one likes you as being old. Let's go downstairs and see what Nick's protégés have dug up for us."

Nick was at the college, but Megan and Keith were in the morgue. They were kissing in one of the exam rooms when Sharyn and Ernie found them. Sharyn jerked aside the green curtain they were hiding behind.

"Sheriff!" Keith jumped to his feet so quickly that Megan fell on the floor. "What are you doing here?"

"Looking for some assistant M.E.s to assist us. Nick told us you could fill us in on anything new you found out about the Mercedes and the second bullet he's had you researching."

Megan got up with a sour look at her partner. She popped her gum loudly and swept her arm towards the door. "Sure thing, Sharyn. Right this way."

"First of all, we found some marks on the back bumper of the Mercedes." Keith showed them the bumper they'd removed from the car. "Nick thinks it's where the machinery the killer used struck the car to push it into the hole. We should be able to ID exactly what did it."

Sharyn examined the bumper. There were six marks,

evenly spaced. Each mark was pushed into the metal. "What do you think did this?"

Megan popped her gum again. "We're checking it out. Probably some kind of heavy equipment. If there were tread marks still left in the ground, we could tell you tomorrow what it was. But without that, it's going to take more time."

"We also found this." Keith held up a large zippy bag that held a piece of what looked like molded clothing. "We're not sure what it is yet or if it's related to the crime scene, but we're working on it, too."

"What about these?" Ernie looked at some receipts in another evidence bag.

"Don't touch those!" Megan jerked the bag from his hand. "You could destroy all the evidence!"

"How about if I just write down the names of the motels on the receipts? I promise not to open the bag."

"I suppose that would be all right. We worked hard to get all of those together, Deputy," Megan scolded. "I don't think you appreciate how exacting it is to work for the medical examiner's office!"

Sharyn went to look at them with him. "These are all eight years old, Ernie. A couple of these motels aren't even there anymore. I don't see what we're going to find out from them."

He took out his pen and paper. "Some of them are still around. It's a long shot, I know. But that's all we've got on this, right?"

She agreed and turned back to Megan and Keith. "What about the body? Do we have a positive ID?"

"We have more than that!" Keith directed her to the far side of the evidence room. "For the record, Dr. Thomopolis told us to officially record the John Doe as Clint Walker. He sent for the med records and they match the metal we found in this dude's leg."

Megan held up the X-rays for her to see. "Imagine going around with a piece of metal in your body that nobody could *see!*"

"We have the second bullet, too," Keith told her. "Surprise! It came from a different gun."

EIGHT

SHARYN TRIED TO look surprised for Keith's sake. It *was* his first ballistics match. She took out her notebook. "Do we know yet what kind of gun it was?"

Keith frowned. "I figure Mr. Walker was probably shot by two different people. I mean, how many people carry two different guns to kill someone?"

"And then buried him alive," Megan finished. "How gruesome is that? Of course, from what I've heard about this man, he was lucky they didn't cut off his—"

"And what kind of gun was that?" Sharyn asked again.

Megan picked up a sheet of paper. "A Ruger semi-automatic Rimfire pistol. MK6, Mark II. Not real unusual. I think Nick has a couple of them. But not your run-of-the-mill type of gun, either. It isn't registered anywhere around here. We've been checking the State and national registries, but no luck so far."

"The strange thing is that it was only a .22." Keith tried again to astound Sharyn. "I could understand the Beretta. Good gun if you want to kill someone, right? But the Ruger? What did the killer hope to do with that? Give him a headache?"

"Where were the different bullets in the body?"

Keith scrambled to find that information. "Here it is. The 9 mm was stopped by a rib. It could have been a ricochet. The .22 was in his left shoulder, nowhere near anything vital."

Ernie finished copying the motel receipts and joined them. "But we also need to know what pushed him into that hole, right?"

"Yeah. We're doing that. It just takes some time to look through the catalogues and compare what we can online." The younger man adjusted his glasses and ran his hand through his thinning hair.

"We're still processing prints. There were a ton of them that didn't belong to the dead guy," Megan said. "We'll get back to you when we've got something on that. Ten-forty. Or whatever it is you guys say."

"Thanks for the information." Sharyn looked at Ernie. "Ready?"

When they were outside, Ernie shook his head. "Are you sure that evidence is safe with those kids?"

"I guess Nick is sure and that's all that matters. And they're not exactly kids, you know? They're both grad students. They've been doing this work for a while."

"I'm just glad I don't have to depend on them for backup." He shuffled through his notes. "Too bad the Bridge Motel burned down last year. Six of the receipts were from there. All with Marti Martin's signature on them. He always had a good memory, if you were *persuasive* enough."

"Didn't I hear someone say he's working out at the Stag Inn Doe?"

"Seems to me I heard that, too. We could check it out. If there's one of these people who might remember a sleazebag like Walker, it would be another sleazebag like Martin."

Sharyn agreed and started the Jeep. "You know, I wasn't any older than Keith and Megan when I became sheriff."

"Yeah. I know. And sometimes, it was *real* scary."

THEY DROVE OUT to the edge of town and parked in the Stag Inn Doe's parking lot. The nightclub was a ramshackle, fire-code-violating nightmare. Because of its location, not quite in the city and right on the county line, it could serve alcohol and strippers to its clientele without any problems with local law enforcement.

The nightclub had been around for as long as anyone could remember. It hadn't missed a single graduating high school class in over fifty years, and frequently hosted parties for senators and judges. It made it difficult to do much about anything that went on out there.

Sharyn's grandfather and her father had both tried unsuccessfully to close it down. She hadn't bothered as yet. There was no point, unless she had something bigger than the usual fights or petty drug busts. The courts tended to look the other way when it came to the Stag Inn Doe.

The present owner met them at the door. "Hey, Sheriff Howard! How's it goin'?"

Duke Beatty was a successful stock-car driver who was well known for his ten-gallon, black cowboy hat and his Cadillac commercials on TV. He was an icon in the area. His daddy once owned a still and sold moonshine for many years. It was rumored that Duke got his start driving fast, running from the police as he took his daddy's 'shine out to sell.

"Hello, Mr. Beatty. We're busy as always. We'd like a few minutes of your time."

"Of course!" He opened the door to the nightclub. "It's not often I see someone from the sheriff's department out here unless there's trouble. Let me buy the two of you a beer."

"We're on duty, Duke," Ernie told him. "Thanks anyway."

Beatty turned his attention on him. "I remember you! You had your bachelor party here last year. How's it goin'? Married life suit you?"

Ernie didn't mind answering. He thought a lot of Duke, like so many other people in Diamond Springs. "Not so good. The wedding was called off."

"No! I hate to hear that! Was it you or her?"

"It was mutual, I guess."

"Well, in that case, I insist you come back for a beer later, on the house." He nudged Ernie in the side with his elbow. "And maybe we can rustle up a petticoat or two, huh?"

Before Ernie could answer, Sharyn intervened. "Mr. Beatty, we're here to see Marti Martin. Is he here?"

"What's the hurry, Sheriff?" He nudged Ernie again. "Women! Always in a hurry for something, huh?"

"You know it." Ernie glanced at Sharyn and sobered

instantly. "Of course, she's right. We need to talk to Mr. Martin."

"Well, I think he's around back counting supplies. You can walk through there." He pointed towards the kitchen. "I don't have anything to hide. Always keep 'em out in front. That's what my daddy taught me."

"Thanks." Sharyn started towards the kitchen. The dark carpet under her feet was like walking on a sticky sponge. She didn't want to think about what had made it that way. If nothing else, the place should be closed to protect the people of Montgomery County from the diseases lurking in that carpet.

As Ernie started to join her, Duke grabbed his arm. "The sheriff is pretty intense, huh? Wouldn't do for a man like me to even think about a woman like her. How does that doctor fella live with that?"

"He's even more intense than her," Ernie confided. "He's from New York, you know."

Sharyn walked through the greasy kitchen, oblivious to their conversation about her. She couldn't believe the AAA rating from the county health department. No amount of cleaning would ever make this place sanitary. What were those inspectors thinking?

Marti was in the back storage area. He was counting the bottles of whiskey and adding the numbers to the count in the laptop that was perched on a folding chair. He was as greasy and disgusting as the kitchen. Working at the Stag Inn Doe was a perfect place for him. It was the only place lower than the Bridge Motel.

"Sheriff!" He dropped a bottle of whiskey when he

saw her. It took him a moment to realize that he wasn't doing anything illegal. "I didn't see you there. You have a way of sneaking up on a man."

"Sorry. How are you, Mr. Martin?"

"I'm fine, thanks." He ran his hand across his closely shaved scalp. "What brings you out to ask?"

Duke stooped to pick up the bottle of cheap whiskey Marti dropped. He rubbed off the dust on his sleeve. "You're lucky this didn't break, boy. Or I'd have taken it out on your backside."

Marti almost dropped another bottle. He fumbled with it then put it gently back into its case. "Duke. What's *everybody* doing out here? I'm just trying to work, you know?"

"Sheriff Howard and Deputy Watkins are here to ask you some questions. I suggest you cooperate completely." Duke nodded to Sharyn and stepped back.

Sharyn felt sure that anything Marti had ever done wrong was small pickings compared to Duke Beatty. But she stayed focused on their particular mission. "We need some information. We're looking for Clint Walker. Do you know him?"

"The name sounds familiar." Marti searched his memory. "Yeah. Nice guy. Nice car. Mercedes, right? Big tipper. Always has a big smile on his face. Yeah, I know him. But I haven't seen him in years."

"Where was he the last time you saw him?" Ernie wondered.

Marti scratched his head. "He was at the motel before it burned down. He was with a woman, of course.

He's *always* with a woman. The man is a chick magnet. I swear I don't know how he does it."

"Any specific woman?" Sharyn asked him. "Or did you ever see him with the same woman twice?"

Duke jumped into the conversation again. "You mean like Brandy?"

"Brandy?" Ernie wrote the name down. "Does she have a last name?"

"I don't ask those kinds of questions." He grinned. "I know Clint, too. That old rascal. Where's he got off to for the last few years anyway?"

Sharyn studied him then shook her head. No. It would be wrong to pin this murder on Duke just to close the Stag Inn Doe. "We got official confirmation this morning. Mr. Walker has been dead for the last eight years. What did you say about Brandy's last name?"

The look on his face was almost comical. "I *really* don't know, Sheriff. Believe me. I'd turn over my own sister if I thought she did something wrong. I always stay on the good side of the law. You know me."

"Yes, Mr. Beatty, I *do* know you. And I think if you don't know Brandy's last name right now, you can find out what it is for me." She smiled at him. "Right?"

"Absolutely! You can count on me. If there's anyone in this county who knows where the dead bodies are buried, it's Duke Beatty."

She raised a cinnamon-colored eyebrow, questioning his choice of words.

He pushed his big black hat farther down on his head and cleared his throat. "I mean, well, chalk that up to bad schooling. I didn't mean the *real* bodies. That was a figure of speech. Of course I don't know where any *real* bodies are buried. Why would I?"

She nodded. "I understand. And you'll have that information for me later today, right?"

"Later today," he agreed. "I'll bring it over myself if I have to."

Sharyn and Ernie went back out of the nightclub through the front door. The rain-soaked morning air was particularly fresh after the stale air inside.

"Smooth." Ernie chuckled. "That was pretty smooth."

She pulled the Jeep out of the parking lot. "I don't think I've ever seen a man so in fear for his life as that man. I wonder what bodies are buried under that place?"

"Old Duke just skirts the law some. He doesn't really break it. It was just a figure of speech, like he said."

"You just can't see past his image," she accused. "He's like the Lone Ranger and all those other anti-heroes. Except that he sells beer and petticoats on the side."

"You think this Brandy person is still around?" Ernie changed the subject. He already knew how Sharyn felt about Duke.

"We'll see. In the meantime, call the hospital and see how the admiral's doing. It'll probably take Duke a while to look through his little black book. Brandy is a pretty common name around here. I think there were five of them in my graduating class in high school."

Ernie's cell phone rang. It was Trudy telling him about an emergency call from Frog Meadow. He thanked her, then told Sharyn, "Well, I guess we get to join the party out at that fence standoff after all. They just started shooting at each other and each of the families is holding members of the other family hostage."

"Anybody hurt?"

"Not that I know of. Maybe we can go out there before they have to call in the National Guard. If anyone can talk to them, I know you can."

"Why Ernie, you'll turn my head with talk like that. And people will know for sure that you and I are officially a couple."

"I already knew about that. Debbie Siler jumped out of her car this morning when I was coming out of your apartment. I believe there'll be something about it in the paper later today."

"Great."

THE BAKER/HONEYCUTT FENCE problem began when Verne Honeycutt decided to have his property surveyed. He wanted to divide up his 150 acres into plots for his six children. The surveyor found that the fence Leroy Baker put up twenty years before was really on Honeycutt land. Verne and his boys started taking the fence down. Leroy and his boys took out their guns to stop them.

Sharyn and Ernie pulled up to the scene along with a paramedic unit.

"They say somebody got shot out here," the lead paramedic told them, "but I'm not going in until I'm sure I won't be shot. Do something, Sheriff."

"That's what I'm here for. You two stay back here until we're sure it's safe."

Joe and Ed met them as they moved closer to the standoff.

"This is a mess, Sheriff," Ed explained. "Nobody's gonna be happy until somebody gets hurt."

Joe nodded. "I can take care of the problem. A couple of mortar shells would do the trick. You have to let them know you're serious."

"That's a little *too* serious, old son," Ernie complained. "I think you've been out here in the sun too long."

"I was only talking about shooting them over their heads," Joe explained.

"I already told you. No mortar shells." Ed looked around.

"Everybody just calm down." Sharyn gathered them together. "Now what happened that made this worse?"

Cari explained how one of the Honeycutt boys crossed the fence and took one of the Baker sisters. They refused to give her back until the Bakers tore down the fence. Then one of the Bakers crossed the fence and took one of the Honeycutt girls back with him.

Ed grinned. "That boy doesn't know what he's in for with one of those Honeycutt girls!"

"Not now, Romeo." Sharyn took off her gun and hat. "I'm going down there to talk to them. This has to end."

Ernie put his hand on her arm. "Not alone. I'll come with you."

"I think one of us won't be as likely to be shot as two of us. And I know Verne Honeycutt pretty well. I went to school with one of his notorious girls. We used to have parties and sleepovers all the time."

"I still don't like it," he disagreed. "Let *me* go if only one of us can go."

"Not this time."

"You mean not *any* time."

Sharyn didn't answer. She held up her hands and started walking into the field. She could see the long, overgrown chicken-wire fence that stretched out between the two pastures. She was on the Honeycutt side. The family was gathered behind a baling machine. The sun glinted on the guns in their hands. "Mr. Honeycutt? It's me, Sharyn Howard."

"I know who you are!" he yelled back. "But you're the sheriff now. You'd best stay out of this. I don't want to be responsible for you getting killed."

She kept walking towards them. "I'm unarmed, Mr. Honeycutt. Is Charlene out here with you?"

"Sharyn?" Charlene's high-pitched voice carried across the field. "They've taken Earlene. You have to help us get her back."

Sharyn remembered Charlene's younger sister from the times she spent at their house. Earlene was the beauty of the family. She would be out of high school now. "I can do that if you put down your guns and talk to me."

"What's to talk about?" Verne demanded. "Tell them to put down their guns and give us back Earlene."

"What about the other girl?" Sharyn asked him. "Do you have one of Leroy's girls?"

There was a commotion and a female voice shouted for help. At the sound, the Baker family started shooting again. Sharyn dropped to the newly planted ground. The smell of fresh dirt and fertilizer was pungent.

"Are you okay out there, Sheriff?" Ernie yelled when the shooting stopped.

The front of her uniform was covered in wet dirt and manure. "Except for a massive dry-cleaning bill." She got up and started walking towards the Honeycutt family again.

Charlene's voice rang out. "You can't shoot her, Daddy. She's one of my best friends. She's like family. Maybe she can help."

Sharyn was grateful to reach the baling machine. She looked at the defiant, dirty faces of the family hiding there. Charlene's older brother, Junior, was holding the Baker girl tightly to his chest. She wasn't more than ten or twelve years old. "I know you've got a problem out here. But I think we can solve it without shooting anybody."

Verne's grizzled face wasn't so sure. "How do you propose to do that? Leroy ain't gonna take down that fence. He won't let me take it down, either. And he's got my Earlene. The only way I can see out of this is to fight our way out, and whatever family still has someone left alive gets his way."

"That sounds a little harsh, Verne. I think maybe we can do it without anybody getting hurt. Let me have the girl. I'll trade her for Earlene and then we can talk about the fence."

Junior shook his head. "No way. She's our insurance that we'll get Earlene back."

"Not if my deputies call in the FBI. You know, we're required to call the Federal Government in any terrorist activity now. And those boys don't come in to talk. They come in with mortar shells and tear gas."

Junior and Verne were suddenly less sure of their position. Charlene took that moment to appeal to her brother and father. "If anybody can take care of this, Sharyn can. Remember when she used to win prizes for her speeches in school? If nothing else, they'll go along with it just to make her stop talking."

Sharyn bit her lip to keep from smiling. It had been a long time since she thought about her high school debate team. The coach always put her in first because she was so long-winded. That was when she decided to be a lawyer. Her father told her it was the only profession that got paid to blow so much hot air. Her debating skills served her well in law school. She never dreamed that she'd use them as sheriff one day.

Verne finally agreed to let her try. He told his son to let the Baker girl go. Junior didn't listen until his father threatened to tie him out in the hog pen.

The girl ran straight to Sharyn. She was crying as she put her arms around her waist and begged her to take her back to her family.

Sharyn smoothed her hair with her hand. "It's going

to be okay now. We're going to walk across the field. Is your father on the other side of that combine?"

"All of them are there."

"What's your name?"

"Mary. I'm named for my grandmother."

"Okay, Mary. My name is Sharyn and I want you to call to your father and tell him what we're going to do. Can you do that?"

Mary nodded and yelled to her father that the sheriff was bringing her home.

There was no response.

Sharyn took Mary's hand. "I guess we're going to have to do this the hard way."

Hand in hand, they started walking across the red clay. There was a break in the fence that would be easy to cross when they came to it. Sharyn knew she made a good target for anybody who was trigger-happy in the Baker family. Most of these people had been squirrel hunting since they were children. And she was a mighty big squirrel.

"Mr. Baker? I'm bringing Mary back to you. I want to resolve this peacefully."

Finally Leroy Baker responded. "Just keep your hands in the air, Sheriff. I promise nobody will shoot you until you get over here."

As promises went, she'd heard better. But she didn't have any choice. She was within shotgun range. She hoped they weren't crazy enough to take a chance on hitting Mary. She'd never forgive herself if the girl came to harm because of her. It was one thing to put herself in danger, another to ask a child to share it.

But they finally reached the combine without an incident. Sharyn glanced back towards the hill where Ernie and the paramedics waited. Now there was a TV news crew, as well. She sighed and focused on the Baker family.

It immediately caught her attention that pretty, eighteen-year-old Earlene wasn't being held against her will. She was sitting beside one of the Baker boys, holding his hand. "Leroy, this can't end good this way. Let me take Earlene back to her family. Then we can talk about the fence."

Earlene gave a little gasp and hid her face in her hands. "I don't want to go back, Sharyn. I love Mark and we want to be married. If I go back, Daddy won't let me see him again."

"That's not fair, Earlene," Sharyn argued. "He thinks the Bakers are holding you hostage. They're willing to kill someone to get you back. I know you don't want them to kill Mark."

Leroy held his old shotgun high. "Just let them try! We aren't afraid of them."

Sharyn played her trump card again. "How about the FBI, Leroy? Are you afraid of them? Because this makes all of you terrorists. We have to call them when something like this happens. I'd hate to see Mary grow up in a prison."

Leroy didn't like the sound of that, but he was stubborn. "I won't live next to them Honeycutts without a fence. They raise Black Angus sometimes and they'd pollute my herd. There's soybeans coming up in that field this year. I don't want Verne accusing my milk cows of eating his soybeans."

"What if you take down the old fence and Verne and his boys put up the new fence?"

"If I do that, I'll lose three feet of my property."

"You've been wrong about that, Leroy. If you don't believe the county surveyor, you can hire your own," Sharyn told him. "But I think you're going to have to live with that loss. The important thing is that Mary has a daddy and a decent place to live."

"Okay." He gave in abruptly. "Me and my boys will take down the fence if Verne and his boys will put up the new one. You're right, Sheriff. Mary is more important than that fence."

Sharyn looked at Earlene. "But none of this is going to happen until you come back with me. Your father won't believe you're not a hostage until you tell him."

"I'll go with her," Mark volunteered, taking Earlene's hand.

"Good boy!" Sharyn commended him. "Sounds to me like the Bakers and the Honeycutts are going to be family anyway. Nobody shoots family."

Mark was as good as his word. He walked so close behind Sharyn that she was afraid he'd knock her over but he went back to the Honeycutts with Earlene. She didn't blame him for worrying about being shot. She just wanted to see the whole thing finished without anyone getting hurt.

Verne wasn't happy with the idea of Earlene and Mark being together. But he went along with the fence plan. "We'll see about the rest. But you got some spine walking over here, son. I like that. Let's go eat something. I'm starved!"

Sharyn walked back to the group on the hill overlooking the fence. The reporters were waiting for her. She gave them a brief statement. She told the waiting paramedics that they could leave. No one had been hurt.

Ernie was relieved to see her, but turned up his nose when she came close. "I'm glad you're safe, Sheriff, but you are *ripe!* Joe, can I ride back with you?"

"The woman saves the day like always," Cari began, "and what does she get? Men giving her a hard time because she smells like manure!"

"I was just kidding," Ernie assured her. "Really. I don't care if she smells like goat cheese as long as she's safe."

Ernie got in the Jeep with Sharyn to "prove" himself and shut the door.

Sharyn sniffed and made a face. "I think I have to go home and take a shower before I go back to work."

"Drop me off at the office before you do. I don't want Debbie Siler seeing you looking like you had a shower and changed clothes with *me* there."

Sharyn's cell phone rang. It was Duke. "Any news yet, Mr. Beatty?"

"I went through all of my business receipts. I think I found her. She went by the name of Brandy Wine when she worked for me. But her real name is Brandy

Butler. She used to live in Indian Creek. That's all I know, Sheriff."

"That's good enough. I appreciate your cooperation."

She closed the phone. "Well, we know who Brandy is now."

"Who?"

"Brandy Butler." She explained further when Ernie's face looked blank. "She owns the Top Notch Beauty Salon over by the college. She cuts my hair. Trudy and my mother go there, too."

"I guess that explains why I don't know who she is."

"I'll drop you off, take a shower, then go and see her. It might be better talking woman to woman." She grabbed a towel from the backseat and put it between her uniform and the seat belt. "Thank goodness it was the front of me instead of the back. I wouldn't be able to get the smell out of these cloth seats."

SHARYN WAVED TO CHARLIE as she left Ernie at the court-house. She drove back to her apartment and parked on the street. There was no sign of any newspaper report-ers watching as she let herself into the building. Ernie was probably just imagining the whole thing.

She had a message on her machine. She listened to it while she waited for the water heater to start work-ing so she could take a shower. It was a little tempera-mental like the rest of the old building.

It was Jill. "Sharyn, Skeeter Johnson is dead. I'm at the prison checking into it. Call me when you can."

Sharyn tried Jill's cell phone but there was no answer. She called the prison and the warden's office confirmed the message. Skeeter was killed in a fight. Maurice, Skeeter's partner, was injured as well but was expected to live. She thanked the office assistant and hung up. Then she punched one of the new purple throw pillows on her sofa.

She was *so* close. Jack must have heard about their meeting and taken care of the problem. There was no way to prove that and nothing she could do to investigate the fight. She was sure an appropriate person would be blamed for Skeeter's death. The status quo would be maintained. Maurice would certainly keep his mouth shut. Jack would be safe.

She showered quickly to wash off the smell of the manure then wrapped a towel around herself, and took the black book out of its hiding place. It might be the only thing that could ever bring Jack down. She had to figure out how to decipher it.

Sitting cross-legged on the bed for an hour, she let the phones ring as she tried again to get some information from the letters and numbers. If she could just break *one* letter, it could give her the key to the whole thing. But no matter what she tried, she couldn't get any of it to make any sense.

Maybe it wasn't as simple as replacing one number or letter with another. Maybe her father was worried about Jack finding the book and deciphering it. But if it was more complex than her rudimentary code-breaking skills, she wasn't sure how she'd ever understand it. She didn't dare ask anyone local for help since she didn't know who was in Jack's pocket.

The code-breaking site she'd found on the internet had suggested that some codes had keys that were based on information. The writer used life experiences, fiction novels, even old songs to put together the code. Sharyn began to write down songs, books and hobbies that were important to her father when she noticed the time. She had to get back to work.

She put the black book back behind the medicine cabinet and put her dirty uniform in a plastic bag. She could drop it off at the dry cleaners later. Her hair was still damp, longer tendrils curling around her shoulders, but it would have to do.

Getting back in her Jeep, she sniffed the interior but it didn't smell like manure. She wished she could say the same thing for her boots. She'd put on another pair but she wasn't sure the ones she'd been wearing could be saved. Still, she couldn't complain. She'd managed to get the two families to work out their differences without shooting each other. That was a pretty good day's work.

She drove over to the beauty salon. It was in an older house that was close enough to the college and the downtown area to draw a large clientele. Brandy was good at what she did and everyone liked her. Sharyn didn't care about her past or what she'd done to buy her salon. She didn't plan to share that information with anyone else unless she had to.

There were no other cars in the small parking area.

It was unusual at that time of day during the workweek to find the place deserted. The door was unlocked. She knew Brandy was there in the salon or her apartment upstairs.

Sharyn looked around until she heard the TV news coming from the small kitchen area in the back of the building. She found Brandy slumped over the table, sobbing. The news reporter was talking about Clint Walker being identified as the dead man found in the cemetery.

Brandy looked up at her with tears streaming down her face. "Sharyn, my husband is dead."

NINE

SHARYN SAT DOWN at the table with her. "You were married to Clint Walker?"

Brandy nodded, still sobbing. Her rose-gold-colored hair was down around her shoulders. Bright red lipstick smudged her lips. "I thought all this time that he left me for another woman. I was so ashamed to lose a man that way. But instead, he was laying up there in that cemetery and I didn't even know. I can't believe I let him down that way after he was so good to me."

It took a few minutes for Sharyn to decide what to tell her. It didn't escape her that, despite the tears, she could be talking to Walker's killer. It seemed more likely that Brandy could do the job than Ladonna. "When were you married?"

"About three months before he disappeared. It wasn't long. But we had a good time, you know? We went to Reno and got married there over a long weekend. Clint really knew how to make a woman feel good about herself. I never met another man like him."

"Did you know Clint was married and had two children?"

Brandy's red-rimmed eyes opened wide in horror. "No! He wasn't married. He never wore a ring. I knew him for a long time. He would've mentioned it. He was always honest with me."

It was a far cry from everyone else's feelings about him. "Brandy, Clint *was* married and he was murdered. We're investigating his death to try to find out who killed him. I'd like you to volunteer to come in and give us your fingerprints to compare to the ones we found in his car. If there's anything else you could tell me that might help, I'd appreciate it."

"I don't know what to say, Sharyn." She sniffed and held a tissue to her nose. "I honestly didn't know he was married. As for my prints, you'll find me in the records. They picked me up a few times at the Stag Inn Doe. That was before I saved up enough to buy this place. Nobody wants that life, you know? It just sort of happens. Clint helped me get out of that. He helped me find myself and get set up. He never made me feel any less for what I did. I loved him. I can't imagine who'd kill him."

Sharyn was inclined to believe her, but she asked her to come in anyway. Brandy had been honest about her past. Maybe she made Walker out to be a little more saintlike than anyone else but wouldn't any woman who was in love with a man?

"So, LET ME GET THIS STRAIGHT," Ernie began when she told him about Brandy. "This ex-stripper marries Walker in Reno, comes back here and gets him to set her up in business, then finds out he's already married and kills him."

"I don't think that's what I said." Sharyn poured herself a cup of coffee. "She struck me as being sincere. I don't think she knew he was married to anyone else. Besides, I don't see where she had any more motive to kill him than Ladonna. Maybe less because their marriage was illegal. If Brandy knew about his first wife, she'd know that, too."

Cari sat back from her computer. "Well, that makes me feel better. I checked in North Carolina for information about him. I didn't think about checking nationally for other marriages."

"He was a busy man," Sharyn agreed. "Take some time and check it out. Use his driver's license and Social Security in case he was married by a few other names. We don't need any other surprises in this case."

Ernie played with his pencil. "You don't like either Mrs. Walker for the murder. You don't believe the admiral was involved even though his gun put one of the bullets into the man. Who *do* you think killed him?"

"I'm not sure. And I'm not ruling any of these people out." She got up and paced the floor. "It just seems to me that neither one of these women had any reason to kill him. I think both of them loved him. Ladonna didn't say anything about his disappearance, just like Brandy, because she believed he was going to come home. Both women would have taken him back."

"The fools," Trudy chimed in. "What were they thinking? A man like that isn't worth any woman's time or effort."

Ed joined them as she was speaking. He didn't say anything as he sat down at his desk.

"Besides being in love with him," Sharyn continued, "neither woman gained anything from his death. Ladonna had to scrape by and finish raising her two children alone. If we suspect Brandy of marrying him to get away from her old life, then she made a mistake killing him. Dead, he was useless to both women."

"I agree," Cari remarked. "If Ladonna or Brandy showed up dead, it would be different. Then you could say one of them turned on the other."

Sharyn glanced at her sharply. "You're right. That could be the whole key to this."

"But neither woman *is* dead," Joe reminded her. "Walker's dead, remember?"

"But we *do* have a dead woman."

"A dead woman that the M.E. has almost ruled a suicide," Marvella added. "I don't know how Nick will feel about you questioning his judgment. Especially with this thing between you and Ernie."

"If we could stay on the subject at hand, please," Ernie growled at her.

"I'm not saying her death *wasn't* a suicide," Sharyn suggested. "But Mr. Percy was right about what he said. You don't have to own the gun to shoot it. What if Vicky was involved with Walker, too?"

Ed groaned. "Take it from me. A man only has so much stamina. This guy couldn't have had another woman! I know *I* couldn't'!"

Trudy frowned at him, but didn't say anything.

Joe laughed. "And that's saying a lot, Ed. But what if he had enough stamina for one more?"

"Vicky Rogers would've been fifteen when Walker was killed," Cari pointed out, looking at her information. "I can't believe a girl that age would find him attractive."

"Stranger things have happened," Ernie assured her.

"Let's take a look at this from another angle." Sharyn decided. "Since Walker's murder would've taken place when Vicky was in high school, we'll need to talk to some of her friends from back then. Maybe some of her teachers knew something about it if she was dating him."

Ernie looked up from his notes. "You *do* realize that you just put the admiral front and center again for Walker's murder? He knew Clint Walker was a skirt chaser who was going after his teenage daughter, so he meets him in the cemetery to warn him away. When he refuses to back off, the admiral shoots him and buries him there."

Sharyn shrugged. "That's true. And if that's how it happened, we need to find out. Vicky's death happened shortly after we discovered the body in the cemetery. Suppose she was young and impetuous when she found out that Walker was already married. She took her father's gun and shot him. She buried him, but eight years later, we dig him up. She's a young woman now with a husband. She's grief-stricken by her actions and afraid that she'll be caught. So she kills herself."

"Or one of Walker's two wives kill her when they

find out that she was sleeping with him eight years ago," Cari added.

"Possible," Joe acknowledged. "But unlikely. That would be a crime of passion. After eight years, the passion wouldn't be there. Even Caison couldn't show *that* in court!"

"Let's check out the connection, if there is one, between Walker and Vicky Rogers. Cari will get us the information about her high school class and her teachers. Joe and Ed, you see what you can do with that. Marvella, let's find out if Vicky had any other relatives who might know about it. We know she doesn't have anyone on the admiral's side, but what about her mother's family?" Sharyn handed out assignments. "Ernie and I will pay another call on Rosemarie Marshal. She said that she and Vicky were friends for years. Maybe she knows something."

"And if everything leads to it being the admiral who killed him?" Ernie persisted.

"We'll deal with that when we get there." Sharyn turned to Cari. "Brandy will be coming in with her marriage license. Get some fingerprints. We'll be back later."

ROSEMARIE MARSHAL LIVED in a small farmhouse a few miles away from where her friend, Vicky, lived. She was carrying a crying toddler when she met Sharyn and Ernie at the front door. Behind her, a four-year-old was watching *Sesame Street*. "Sheriff! What brings you out here this time?"

"I can see you're busy, Mrs. Marshal, but I have a few questions I'd like to ask you about your friend, Vicky."

"What's going on?" her husband asked. "Is there a problem, Sheriff?"

"This is my husband, Frank." Rosemarie introduced them. She handed him the baby. "She wants to ask me some questions about Vicky."

Frank nodded. "I don't see what else there is to say. The woman was a whacko. She was too upset about her own problems to care that she was leaving her sick father and her husband to fend for themselves."

Sharyn nodded. "I appreciate your opinion, Mr. Marshal. But we have to follow up on all the angles."

He shushed the baby. "Waste of my tax money, ma'am. But you did a fine job on breaking up that family feud going on today. I'll watch the kids, Rosie. You can talk to them in the sunroom so you don't have to talk around the TV."

Sharyn and Ernie sat with her on the bright green-and-white-striped patio furniture. The sun was hot, slanting through the overhead windows.

"Would you like something to drink?" Rosemarie asked them.

"No, thanks," Sharyn replied. "You said that you and Mrs. Rogers had been friends for years."

"Since junior high when my parents moved here. We had a lot of classes together. We became friends right away."

"Did Mrs. Rogers ever date a man named Clint Walker?" Sharyn studied the other woman's face.

"You mean the man you found buried in the car?" Rosemarie pointed to the front page of the paper that was lying on the footstool. An early photo of the dead man was prominently displayed. "Vicky was a cheerleader in high school. You know what that means, Sheriff. She had her pick of any guy she wanted. That man in the car would've been pretty old. I can't imagine her having anything to do with him."

Ernie leaned forward and picked up the paper. "He doesn't look familiar to you?"

Rosemarie looked at the paper again. "Not much to look at, was he? I don't think Vicky would've been impressed by him at all. She dated Chad Stevens. He was the quarterback who went on to play one season with the Panthers in Charlotte. He was injured, but he was gorgeous. Still is."

"The same gun that killed Mrs. Rogers shot Mr. Walker," Ernie explained. "Her father had that gun registered to him for the last twenty years. We believe there was a connection between them. We don't want to put you on the spot, Mrs. Marshal, but we have to find out the truth about this."

Rosemarie nibbled nervously at one of her pink fingernails. "Are you sure? I mean, are you sure that the same gun shot the man in the car?"

"Very sure," Sharyn answered. "The medical examiner is about to rule Vicky's death a suicide. She killed herself just after it was announced that we found the body in the car. We didn't know it was Mr. Walker until yesterday. But we think Vicky knew."

"And you think Vicky killed him all those years ago then killed herself *now?*" Rosemarie laughed. "I don't believe it. She wasn't like that. She'd changed since she moved out here. She didn't want to give up her job. She didn't want to take care of her father. They were never close, you know. She and her mother were close. I don't know how a bullet from the same gun got into that man, but it would be more likely that the admiral murdered him than Vicky. Vicky wouldn't hurt another living soul."

There wasn't much more to say. Sharyn and Ernie listened to her ramble on about high school memories, then excused themselves.

"Thanks for your time, Mrs. Marshal." Sharyn extended her hand. "Here's my card. If you think of anything else, please give me a call. I'm sorry about your friend."

Rosemarie shrugged. "I like to think she's gone on to a better place. She wasn't happy here anymore. Too many things had happened and she just couldn't live with herself."

"I warned you it could go this way," Ernie said as they walked out the door together. "You know, maybe Mrs. Marshal is right about her friend not shooting Walker. It sure makes more sense to me that way. Maybe she knew that her father killed him and didn't want to go through that when it all came out."

Sharyn opened the driver's door. "You can tell you weren't a girl with a best friend in high school."

"No." He laughed. "I would've made a mud-ugly

girl. I'm sure I wouldn't have had *any* friends. What's your point?"

"Best friends in high school tell each other everything. Particularly about the boys in their lives. Secretly dating an older man who had a Mercedes wouldn't be something a fifteen-year-old would keep to herself. Either Mrs. Marshal is lying about being Vicky's best friend. Or she's lying about not knowing that Vicky spent time with Walker."

"That's *if* we can find any other evidence besides your gut feeling that Vicky dated Walker," he reminded her. "So far, it all seems to point towards the admiral for me."

"But if Walker *wasn't* dating Vicky, the admiral had no reason to kill him," Sharyn reasoned. "Mrs. Marshal was pretty quick to pin the shooting on him, wasn't she?"

"No one wants to believe that their friend is capable of murder."

"I suppose not," she agreed. "And it's always easy to blame the parents."

"But I agree with you that something's not right about the whole thing. Maybe someone else found some evidence one way or another. I just hope it wasn't Marvella. I don't think I can work with her if she solves the case. That woman might cause me to take early retirement!"

Sharyn laughed and turned onto the Interstate. "Too much ego for you?"

"Too much *everything* for me."

Sharyn's phone rang. It was Cari. "I'm getting ready to leave for the night. But I have a list of all of the people in the county who bought a Ruger pistol here in the past ten years. Some of them are gun dealers. One of them is the ME for Montgomery County. I didn't see any familiar names that might help with the case."

"Thanks. That doesn't include the guns bought and sold privately, of course. But it seems like a pretty exotic gun for this area. Maybe we'll have some luck tracking it down."

They drove back to town and picked Nick up at the hospital.

Sharyn invited Ernie to dinner again and he accepted. "I need to run by the office for just a minute, if that's okay."

"Sure. We're not in any hurry, are we, Nick?"

Nick mumbled something in reply but she couldn't understand what he said. Sharyn decided not to ask again. They waited while Ernie went into the office.

"Wouldn't you like to ask Charlie if he wants to come to dinner, too?" Nick waved to the old man at the gate. "He looks pretty hungry."

She rested her head against the side window. "Don't start. Ernie needs us right now. We can't let him down."

"Could we just decide on *when* he needs us? Say for instance, he lives with you. We could eat dinner without him. Or he doesn't live with you and we eat dinner with him every night."

Before she could answer, Ernie came out of the building with a dazed expression on his face. "Annie called.

She invited me over for supper to talk. I guess you'll have to go on without me."

Sharyn smiled. "That's wonderful! I hope you two get back together."

"I hope so, too. But let's not get too far ahead of ourselves." He glanced at Nick. "Try to have a good time without me. I know it will be hard with the two of you being alone together and all."

"We'll try," Nick promised. "Seriously Ernie, good luck. Don't take no for an answer."

It was such a beautiful evening that Nick and Sharyn decided to take their dinner and eat down by the lake. They picked up Thai food from a corner restaurant near her apartment and sat at the base of the old suspension bridge. At one time, the bridge was going to span the lake but its builders ran out of money. Now it was just a memory of the town's heyday. Since the motel burned down nearby, it was quiet. The county commission was even talking about building a park there to preserve the historical partial bridge.

"I saw you on TV this afternoon," Nick said, looking out at the lake. "You were out in the field when that family started shooting. For a minute, when you hit the ground, I wasn't sure if you were shot. I don't think I took a breath until you got up again."

"I was fine. Smelly, but fine."

"*You* knew that. I didn't." He used his chopsticks to get the last of the noodles out of the white cardboard box. "Don't you think you could endanger someone else's life once in a while? Let Ernie walk into the field where people are shooting, or let Ed fall out of the second-story window and barely miss hitting the rocks."

She decided not to take him seriously. "I've tried to get them to do that stuff. They just won't. So I don't have any choice. You'll just have to stop watching TV."

He put his food down and put his arms around her, drawing her back against his chest. "I wouldn't care except that I get this terrible pain around my heart when I think you've been shot or stabbed or buried under rubble. My doctor says that my heart is already like I've had ten heart attacks. I don't know how much more it can stand."

She kissed him. "Well, for the sake of your heart, I'll try not to let TV cameras take my picture when I'm doing something dangerous."

He pulled back and looked into her eyes. "I love you, Sharyn. I'm a lot older than you. I plan on dying *before* you. Please don't take that away from me."

"I love you, too, Nick." She tried not to laugh. "I don't plan on dying anytime soon."

"Seriously." His eyes held hers. "I know you have a dangerous job. Just be careful, huh? Otherwise, I *will* put in to become a deputy."

"Like I'd approve *that!*" Her pager went off and she glanced at the message. "It's Aunt Selma. She wants me to go out there tonight. It must be important. She always calls and leaves me a message."

"I'll drive out with you," he offered.

"I thought you had to finish grading your test papers."

He tossed their trash into the bright orange can nearby. "Even I get to play hooky once in a while. Besides, Selma is bound to have some kind of homemade pie or cake that will chase down that Thai food just right."

SELMA HOWARD OPENED her front door and invited them in. Her long, curly red hair was loose on her shoulders. It was the same color as Sharyn's but streaked with white. "Looks like a storm is coming. Good thing. It's been too hot. A storm will cool things down for a while. Hello, Nick. How have you been?"

"Just fine, Selma." He got the same hug that Sharyn got a moment before. "How about you?"

"I can't complain." She dragged them inside and put some chamomile tea on to boil. "I'm glad you could come out right away, Sharyn. I know you're busy. I saw you on TV with the Honeycutts. Nice job."

"Thanks." Sharyn waited for her aunt to tell her what was going on. It wasn't like Selma to make small talk when she had something to say. "How's Sam?"

"I'm well, thanks." Sam Two Rivers came in behind them. "I just finished adjusting Selma's lightning rod. The storm coming up will be a bad one. The house needed protection."

His face was almost the same deep orange-brown color as the center of a cedar tree. It was lined and watchful but his black eyes sparkled beneath his thick, iron-gray hair tied in a ponytail at the nape of his neck. He'd worked with wild animals on his own for years before accepting Bruce Bellow's invitation to help with animal control for the county.

Sharyn didn't ask how he knew about the storm. Sam was a shaman and knew things that almost always made her uncomfortable. He'd once cured her head cold by putting his hand on her head and mumbling a few words. She didn't know how it worked but she felt better after he was done. He talked to the bears and the wolves in the mountains, too.

Now he looked at her, studying her face closely. She wanted to walk away but knew he'd follow her. He was going to say whatever was on his mind anyway. She waited for the pronouncement.

"You're not sleeping," he said finally. "Too many secrets."

She looked away. He saw too much. She didn't want to talk about the book she found.

"And you." Sam focused on Nick. "Get some sun! You're starting to look like a corpse! You spend too much time in that basement, surrounded by dead people."

"Thanks, Sam," Nick responded. "You're right. I need a vacation. I was thinking about Florida."

Selma gave them each a slice of fresh strawberry pie and a cup of tea. "Go talk about manly things while I talk to Sharyn, hmm?"

Both men complied. Sam offered to show Nick the orphaned puma kittens he'd found.

"Sam's a dear but he tends to hang around a lot." Selma got out two more cups and squeezed honey into them. "Is Nick that way?"

"It's hard to say since we work together." Sharyn got herself and her aunt some pie. She'd have to work out an extra half hour tomorrow but she knew it was worth it. "Although he *does* go on about me being with Ernie too much."

"That's one of the problems with working together." Selma sighed and brought the cups of tea to the table. "I heard from Kristie yesterday. She's coming down for Memorial Day. She also told me about spying on Jack. I can't believe you asked her to do that, Sharyn."

"I didn't *ask* her to spy on Jack," Sharyn defended. "I asked her to leave him alone. She thinks she's doing this for me, but I've told her that I don't want her there. She won't listen."

"What about Jill?" Selma went on. "Was that a mutual decision or one she made by herself?"

"How did you know about Jill?"

"Jack called me."

"What?" Sharyn couldn't believe it. "Why did he call *you?*"

"Because he wants me to give you a kick in the pants and tell you to leave him alone." Selma sipped her tea. "I've warned you half a dozen times not to keep on after him. Jack can play hardball."

"Was he threatening Kristie or Jill?" Sharyn questioned. "Did he actually threaten them over the phone? We could get him for that."

"You know better than that." Selma sighed. "He's played this game a lot longer than you, Sharyn. He won't be brought down that easily."

"Everyone makes mistakes."

They were huddled over their steaming cups in the old kitchen where several generations of the Howard family had grown up. Selma was the last. She'd cared for her father and mother and stood alongside her brother's grave as his body was lowered into the ground. Sharyn respected her and valued her advice.

"I don't know if you've ever wondered why I never married." Selma looked into the depths of her cup. "There was a man once. I won't tell you his name. You'd go out on the internet or something and look him up. It doesn't matter anyway. He and I were going to be married. We were very young. For some reason, Jack took a fancy to me. He wouldn't leave me alone. I didn't know what to do. So I told my special man."

Sharyn didn't know if she'd ever heard that tone in Selma's voice. It was terrible and frightening, like a storm that could spill out at any time. Thunder rumbled outside around them.

"I realized my mistake right away. He went to Jack and threatened him. The next day, someone took a shot at him. The bullet grazed his cheek. He wasn't seriously injured but I knew it was only a warning. I let him go and agreed to go out with Jack if he'd leave him alone. I *knew* what happened. And I thought if I humored Jack that he'd eventually get tired of me."

"What happened?"

Selma drew a shaky breath. "Jack *did* get tired of me. But it was too late. The man I wanted to be with had joined the Army when I told him we had to break up. He was killed overseas. And that's why I've always lived alone. Not because I'm still worried about Jack, but because I never met another man, until Sam, that I loved as much."

They sat together silently for a few moments. Each woman was lost in her own thoughts while the storm grumbled closer to Diamond Springs.

"I know that Jack is obsessed with you," Selma finally said. "That's why he toys with you about trying to find things out about him. It's like a game with him. He'd have anyone else killed. But you can push him too far. Your father made that mistake."

Sharyn sat up straight. "What do you know about it."

"Nothing I can prove. Your father found something that he thought was going to put Jack away for a long time. I don't know what it was. He threatened Jack with it unless he stepped down as DA. But Jack had some old gambling debts that he'd paid off for T Raymond. He thought that would keep your father quiet. But we both know T Raymond was too stubborn to let Jack blackmail him."

Sharyn desperately wanted to tell her aunt about the book she'd found. But she was afraid that it might endanger her. So instead, she told her about Skeeter Johnson.

"You'd better call your lawyer friend away from this," Selma warned. "He probably wouldn't hurt Kristie because of you. But I don't know about Jill. Just the fact that he's aware that she's doing some snooping is bad enough."

"But we have to take a stand somewhere, Aunt Selma. This isn't about kid's stuff anymore. Jack needs to be stopped. He's in a position of even more power now. Imagine what he could do with it."

Selma reached out and took Sharyn's hand. "I *am* imagining it. I know what it's like to lose someone you care about. I don't want to lose you, too."

Sharyn hugged her, the sweet scent of lavender enveloping her as she pressed her cheek against Selma's. "You and Nick. Sometimes I feel like I'm being smothered in people worrying about me. I'll be fine. But I have to see this through. I'll talk to Jill. I don't like it that Jack knows about her work, either."

"I'm proud of you, honey. Just don't let that badge go to your head." Selma poured herself another cup of tea. "I think I hear Sam and Nick coming back now. Either the pie is gone or they just can't stand being away from us any longer."

"I don't know about Sam. But Nick's pie was gone a minute after they left." Lightning crashed close by and the old house shuddered around them. "I guess we should get back before this gets any worse. Thanks for telling me about Jack calling you."

"He did it just to taunt you," Selma warned. "He knew you wouldn't like it."

Sharyn sat quietly in the kitchen. She could almost hear her father and Selma as children playing on the stairs and in the big rooms. The Howard homestead was over 200 years old. It creaked and moaned in the night. But she loved it here better than any place else

JOYCE & JIM LAVENE

on earth. Her heart was here. Jill had helped them keep it a short time back when the county was going to put part of the new Interstate through it. Despite her thirst for information to use against Jack, Sharyn didn't want to see Jill hurt.

Nick and Sharyn left Selma's house just before the rain hit. The storm rolled over them as they reached the outskirts of town. Slashing rain made it difficult to see and high winds blew debris onto the road. More than once, Sharyn had to swerve to miss a tree branch that would've wrecked her Jeep.

Diamond Springs was worse. Power was out and tree limbs were everywhere. The drought and fires from last year had left the big oaks vulnerable to the high winds. Sharyn brought the Jeep to a quick stop when they saw one of the new, blue police cars with a massive oak lying across it. The car was in the middle of Main Street, the headlights still on.

"Someone might be inside," Sharyn said to Nick as she looked for her poncho in the backseat. "Call nine-one-one and get the emergency workers out here. Tell them to bring their chain saws."

TEN

"Phones are down. I can't raise anyone on the radio," Nick shouted through the howling wind. "I'm going to walk over to dispatch. Is anyone inside the car?"

"Yeah. I'll stay with him until someone gets here," she yelled back.

Lightning cracked close by and the rain came down harder. Thunder shook the street like an earthquake.

"I'll be back as soon as I can," he promised.

Sharyn looked at the unconscious man again. He barely looked old enough to be an officer. She recognized him from a few of her encounters with the police force.

He was trapped between the roof and the floorboard of the squad car. The weight of the tree had crushed the car around him. They would have to cut up the tree and move it, then pry him out of the car.

He groaned and she crouched down beside him, pushing the folded door out of the way. "It's okay. Help is coming. You're going to be all right."

He opened pain-filled eyes and stared at her. "What happened? I remember the storm and then an explosion. Was there a bomb?"

"No. Just a big old tree whose roots couldn't hold it

up anymore." The rain began pelting him in the face and she shifted position so that she was shielding him from the worst of it with her poncho. "What's your name?"

"Terry Bartlett."

She looked at his face again. "You're the manager's son from the Regency Hotel, right? I'm Sharyn Howard. I know your father. He's a good man."

"Yeah. He doesn't speak quite as highly of you, Sheriff." He groaned and tried to move.

"Keep still, Terry. We'll have to get you out of here carefully. There's about a thousand pounds of tree on you right now. Let's not make it any worse. Are you in pain?"

He gritted his teeth and shook his head. It was the only part of him that wasn't crushed inside the car. "Well, a little, maybe."

Lightning struck a satellite dish on the outside of the courthouse. Sharyn shifted again as the rain changed direction. "Well, Terry, in our job, some people aren't going to like you. No matter what you do. I'm sure you'll find that out as you go along."

"I'm already finding that out," he agreed with an attempt at a smile. "I had to search a guest at The Regency for drugs the other day. My dad wasn't happy about it."

"But he'll like it when there's an unruly guest he can't handle," she promised. "And those things count, too."

He stared up at her. "You're different than I thought you'd be."

"How's that?" she asked, eager to distract him.

"Not as tough. More human than Chief Tarnower makes you out to be."

She laughed and wished someone would hurry with help. She couldn't see anything of Terry's body but there was a thin line of blood seeping out from under the car seat. "It's early yet. At midnight, I change."

Terry moaned even though he bit his lip to try and keep it in. The weight of the tree groaned with him as the branches shifted and the car continued to be crushed further down. "You should go. You could be hurt out here, too."

"I'm not going to leave you." She couldn't hold his hand but she touched his face.

"Thanks, Sheriff."

"They'll be here soon. That's one of the good things about living in a small town. Help doesn't take too long and when they come, they come out in force. Just hang in there, Terry. Did I ever tell you about the time I was inside a cabin and it collapsed around me?"

She kept talking to him even when help finally came. The rain soaked through her poncho and her clothes underneath it. Her teeth chattered but she kept on talking. Nick offered to take her place as they began to chainsaw the tree into pieces. When she refused, he wrapped a blanket around her and got her some hot coffee.

Because the car frame couldn't stand any more weight being put on it, the workers had a tough time sawing the tree into moveable sections. They had to bring in a small crane from the construction site on Eighth Street to get the blocks of wood off the car. Paramedics hooked up an IV to Terry's arm but that was all they could do until he was free.

Finally, Terry's parents arrived and tearfully watched from the sidelines of the crowd that had gathered in the rain. The storm passed, leaving days of cleanup behind. Power was restored to most of the area before they were finally able to free the young officer from the police car.

"Thank you for staying with him, Sheriff." Mr. and Mrs. Bartlett shook her hand as she moved away to let the emergency workers do their job. "Does he seem— Do you think he'll be all right?"

"I'm not a doctor," Sharyn answered. "But he's strong. I hope he'll recover."

Nick put his arm around her shoulder. "Let me drive you home. Maybe you can still get a few hours' sleep. You know what Sam said."

"Thanks. My hands and feet are numb." She looked back as they used the jaws of life to free Terry from the crushed car. "I hope he'll make it."

"I hope so, too." He kissed the side of her head. "You were more than a sheriff tonight. You were a heroine in the classic sense."

She laughed and cuddled closer to him for warmth. "Maybe they'll sing stories about me around the fire one day."

"Sheriff?" Roy's grating voice called her from the crowd.

"Don't look back," Nick advised. "Maybe he'll go away."

But he pushed up in front of them, blocking their way

back to the Jeep that was still parked in the middle of Main Street. "I want a word with you, Sheriff Howard."

Sharyn stopped and nodded. "Chief."

He took off his hat and offered her his hand. "Thanks for helping my boy out. Maybe there *is* room for improvement in our working relationship."

"Thanks, Roy." She shook his hand, surprised at the gesture.

He cleared his throat. "Now you'd better get your vehicle off the street. Just because you're the sheriff doesn't give you the right to park in the middle of a *city* street. That's *my* jurisdiction!"

"We're on our way." Nick pulled Sharyn along with him. "Nice seeing you again, Chief."

"Well, *that* was a surprise," she quipped quietly. "I thought he was going to give us a ticket."

"If he did," Nick opened the door for her, "we could've torn it up. Then we could've had Ernie hit him again."

SHARYN WENT INTO the office a few hours later to a round of applause from her deputies. There were fresh flowers, free doughnuts, and coffee donated by a few shops in town when word of the rescue reached TV viewers that morning.

She took a bow and produced the big dry-erase board she'd brought with her. "I couldn't sleep, so I thought we'd hit the ground running this morning and figure out this murder case."

"Wow!" Ed looked at the board as he ate a chocolate-covered Krispy Kreme doughnut. "These doughnuts are really fresh!"

Cari put her purse down. "Why can't anything be simple?"

"Are we still focusing on the Rogers woman?" Joe asked. "Wouldn't we be better off focusing on who killed Walker?"

"What do we have to work with on his death?" Sharyn responded. "Two women who were both married to him but loved him and stood nothing to gain by his death. A pack of angry men who thought he was scum, but none of them seem to have been directly affected by his womanizing."

Ed interrupted. "But maybe we just haven't talked to the right man yet. Knowing your wife is fooling around can be a powerful motive to kill someone. There's been times when I—"

"Can we have a conversation about this man without you relating it to your life?" Cari asked him.

"I agree with you, Ed." Sharyn stopped them before the conversation got ugly between the two ex-lovers. "But this happened eight years ago. No one even missed him except his wives. The likelihood that someone was way out there and saw what happened isn't good. Finding out who killed Walker from that angle is coming up against a dead end. If we can find the link between the two shootings, the rest of it might fall into place."

"Good morning!" Ernie sang out as he skipped down the basement stairs. "Sorry I'm late, but I had a home-cooked breakfast this morning."

"What are you talking about, Ernie?' Ed demanded. "And why are you so darn chipper?"

"Yeah," Joe added, "in this group, that could be a liability."

Sharyn was happy for Ernie but didn't want to get off track. "We're just having a briefing about Vicky Rogers, if you'd like to sit in."

"Okay. I had dinner with Annie last night," Ernie said quickly. "We're just taking it one day at a time but she's asked me to move in to the guesthouse on her property. And she made me breakfast this morning!"

There was a wave of applause, whistling, and foot stomping that accompanied his words. Ed, Nick and Joe slapped him on the back. Trudy and Sharyn hugged him.

Cari walked up to him and put out her hand. "I hope this means we can be friends again?"

Ernie ignored her outstretched hand and hugged her. "We've *always* been friends, young'un. I think I see that now. Sorry I was such a jerk."

Because Ernie was out of contact last night, everyone had to tell him about Terry Bartlett's rescue. There was another round of applause and conversation.

Sharyn waited until the uproar died down. "*Now* can we get on with it?"

Ed and Joe discussed the people they'd spoken to from Vicky Rogers's high school days. So far, there was nothing about her dating an older man.

"We still have about ten names that Cari found for us," Joe said. "There were a few dead ones on the list and a few out of state that we're gonna call today. But everyone remembers Vicky Vendicott as the golden girl. She had everything and did everything."

Ed continued, "If anything, people were amazed that she didn't marry Chad Stevens and that she even looked at Stan Rogers."

"Have you talked to the football hero?" Sharyn asked. "It seems like he would've noticed if his girl-friend was dating another man."

"He was unavailable for comment." Ed made a face. "Nothing worse than a has-been celebrity."

She nodded. "I think we should pay another visit to Stan Rogers. If Vicky knew him in high school, he might have some information for us. Cari is on patrol with Ed today. Joe, I'll let you work on the rest of that list. Marvella can't pull a double again today, but she's starting work early so that she can talk to Vicky's aunt."

"You got it, Sheriff." Cari took her gun out of the drawer.

"Ernie and I will talk to Stan and see if we can get some information from the ex-celebrity. I think that's all." Sharyn checked her notes. "Except that I'd like to solve this by Memorial Day. And Aunt Selma has in-vited all of you out to the farm for her annual beginning-of-summer celebration."

While everyone else was getting ready to go and Trudy was answering the phone, Nick sat down with Sharyn at her desk. "How are you? You didn't get any sleep, did you?"

"No. But I'm fine. A little hoarse from trying to talk

over that storm, but I'll live. I suppose you didn't hear anything about Terry?"

"I must be getting as good as Ernie." He patted himself on the back. "I checked with the hospital before I got here. He's out of surgery. They expect him to recover. It's going to take some time with all of his injuries. He's lucky to be alive."

"Thanks for checking."

"I'd like to release Walker's body to his wife. She's driving me crazy asking for it and I'm done with him."

"Which one? Brandy brought her marriage license over and it's legitimate."

"Ladonna. She was the only *legal* Mrs. Walker. She wants to give her man a proper burial and she has Talbot breathing down my neck to do it. If you don't have a problem with it, I'll release him today."

"That's fine."

"What about Vicky Rogers? Stan doesn't have a lawyer, but I feel sorry for him. He wants to bury his wife."

"Not yet. Let's finish this part of the investigation. It shouldn't take more than a day or two. I don't want to ask to have her exhumed because we need something else. And thanks for holding off on an official statement about her death."

"No problem. I don't want to look stupid calling it a suicide if it isn't one." He touched her face. "You look exhausted. Maybe you should take that vacation in Florida with me."

"Once this case is over, I'm going hiking up in the

mountains," she promised. "No cell phone, no computer, no handcuffs. Want to come?"

He considered her offer. "I don't care about any of that other stuff. Can I bring my new shotgun?"

"Sure. But you can't load it. No firearms allowed up there in the park."

"You'll be carrying your revolver," he complained. "And I think it'll be loaded."

"That's why I'm the sheriff. If you want to do that, you can challenge me in the next election.

He kissed her quickly. "That's okay. I'll talk to you later. The kids are still stumbling around looking for whatever equipment pushed the Mercedes into that hole. I'm going to give them a hand. I'll let you know if we come up with anything."

ERNIE AND SHARYN drove out to the farm where Stan Rogers was staying with his sister. Ernie spent the whole time talking about how great Annie looked and how happy he was that they were back together. Sharyn wasn't sure if an ecstatic Ernie was any better than a morose Ernie. Both were slightly annoying. She'd be happy when he was back to his normal self.

Stan Rogers told them that he wasn't able to go home yet. "I keep thinking about her being dead in there. I might have to sell the place. What does a single man need with a whole house anyway?"

Sharyn looked at his grief-stricken face. He was haggard and didn't look like he'd shaved or bathed since his wife's death. She thought he might even be wearing the same clothes. "I'm sure your wife wouldn't want you to lose everything because of her death."

"Well, she could've thought about that instead of killing herself!" His voice was raw with emotion. "She was the only good thing that ever happened to me, Sheriff. Look at me. I'm a high school dropout who works second shift at a cotton mill that's going out of business. I'm a loser. I'm sure the admiral told you that."

"Vicky must not have thought you were a loser," she reminded him. "She married you. And from what I hear, she had her choice of plenty of men."

Stan lit a cigarette and blew smoke into the air.

"I asked you not to smoke in the house," his sister's voice rang out from the kitchen. "Please take it outside."

They walked outside together and sat on the front steps.

"Vicky was pretty popular in high school," Stan told them. "I don't know what she saw in me. But I loved her. She was like a beautiful angel. Maybe that's why she couldn't stay with me."

"The two of you dated in high school?" Ernie asked.

"No. We knew each other. But it wasn't until she graduated from tech school that we started dating. We were only married a few months before the admiral had his stroke. Then we had to move out here and she had to give up her job to take care of him. Between the two of them living so close by, it was like being caught between Satan and the spawn of Satan."

Sharyn glanced at Ernie then asked, "Satan being the admiral, who was the spawn?"

"Rosie." He inhaled another puff of smoke. "She was always there, always giving Vicky a hard time about something."

"Something like what?" Ernie wondered.

Stan crushed his cigarette on the ground. "You know those TV commercials where nothing is ever good enough for the woman? That's the way Rosie was with Vicky. Vicky was always trying to live up to Rosie's standards. That's probably what drove her crazy. She started taking that medicine for depression earlier this year. I don't think she would've needed it if it wasn't for the admiral and Rosie."

"Did Vicky ever talk about dating an older man in high school?" Ernie came to the point. "Maybe she mentioned that he left her or that they broke up?"

Stan shook his head. "I don't think so. I remember her dating that football boy and the senior class president. That's about it. I can't imagine the admiral letting anybody too much older date her. It was tough enough for *me*. Who are you talking about anyway?"

"Clint Walker." Sharyn waited for his reaction. Telling him her theory was a calculated risk.

"You mean the dead man in the car?"

"There was a connection between Vicky and Mr. Walker. They were both shot with the same gun."

He laughed. "That doesn't surprise me any. That gun belonged to the admiral, you know. He gave it to her when I started working second shift and she was alone at the house after dark. I think you might have your connection there, Sheriff. If a married man was sniffing around after Vicky when she was in school, the admiral wouldn't have thought twice about shooting him."

Ernie smiled at Sharyn and shook his head.

She got up from the stairs. "Thanks for your time, Mr. Rogers. If you think of anything else, please give me a call."

Stan stood up beside her. "Will you ask that coroner to give up her body? It's bad knowing she's laying down there. She needs to be buried."

"I'll do what I can."

"I hate to say I told you so," Ernie began as soon as they got in the Jeep. "But I told you so. I don't think there's any question about how that bullet got into Walker. He flirted with the wrong female and her daddy shot him."

"Twice? With two different guns? Then buried him?"

He shrugged. "Let's face it, Sheriff. No one liked this man. But like you said this morning, we haven't found any other man who could be upset enough to do something like this. *Except* Admiral Vendicott."

Sharyn hated to admit it, but what he said made sense. "Let's go over and talk to the football hero before we hang the admiral. You may be right. He may be responsible, and Vicky's death was a result of her being stressed out and reaching her breaking point when she knew her father was going to get caught for his crime."

Ernie grinned like a possum. "Well, this is just my day, isn't it? Not that I don't deserve it after a long dry spell. The only thing anyone could do to ruin it is to make me do something stupid again that changes what I have with Annie."

She turned the Jeep into the parking lot of one of the new office complexes at the edge of town. "You don't need my help with that, my friend. You can do that all by yourself."

"Ouch!" He looked wounded. "That was downright mean."

CHAD STEVENS WAS a dynamo of a man. Even after losing his contract with the Panthers, he still pushed himself into a lucrative franchise, selling concession rights to auditoriums and stadiums across the county.

Sharyn and Ernie didn't have any trouble locating his office on the second floor. There was a life-size cardboard cutout of him in his number 12 jersey.

"I think this is the place." Ernie thumped the cutout.

They walked into the office. The walls were tastefully covered with pictures from Chad's short professional football career. Everything else in the room seemed like an afterthought.

Sharyn pulled out her badge. "We'd like to see Mr. Stevens, please."

The secretary looked up at them and wrinkled her nose before she refocused on the computer screen. "Mr. Stevens is in conference. He can't see you right now."

"We'll wait."

"He's going to be in conference all day."

"We'll wait."

"He probably won't have time to see you. He's catching a plane to Houston later. You should call back for an appointment."

"Tell Mr. Stevens that Sheriff Howard is here to see him on an urgent legal matter. If he can't make time for me here, I'll have to ask him to come to my office."

Ernie smiled at the secretary. "Trust me, he doesn't want to come to her office."

A little frazzled, the secretary called into the inner office. She spoke to her boss and nodded, then put the phone down. "Mr. Stevens can see you now."

"What about his conference?" Sharyn asked just to see the girl squirm.

"That's just what he pays me to say. Don't blame me!"

Six-foot-three, broad shoulders, shaggy bleached blond hair, Chad Stevens sat behind an oversize glass desk. He was tossing a football from hand to hand. "Hello, Sheriff. How's it goin'?"

"It's early yet, Mr. Stevens. It's hard to say." She put her hand into his outstretched one after he jumped to his feet.

He rubbed his hand across hers. "You have very soft hands. I thought they might be callused from all of the things you do as sheriff. I saw you yesterday on TV. You're very photogenic. Ever consider a career in the media? I have a lot of connections."

Ernie snickered behind her back but didn't say anything.

"Thanks, Mr. Stevens. I'm happy where I am. I'd like to ask you a few questions about Vicky Vendicott."

He sat back down and put his feet on the desk. "Shoot." He laughed as he looked at her gun. "Sorry. Not really. Vicky Vendicott?"

"Yes. I don't know if you read it in the newspaper, but Vicky is dead." Sharyn sat down in a chair at the front of the desk.

"You're kidding? What happened to her?"

"We're not sure yet," Ernie hedged. "We're investigating her death."

"Well, I didn't do it. I just got back from Chicago this morning. I've been gone for two weeks."

Sharyn smiled. "We weren't suggesting that you were responsible. We're looking into Vicky's past. Especially high school. We were told the two of you were pretty tight for a while."

Chad looked anxiously between the sheriff and her deputy. "We *were*. But she married some loser after school. I haven't seen her in years. I don't know what I can tell you about her. She was gorgeous. She was smart. *Too* smart. Her father was this crazy man who kept coming out to the car and threatening me with his gun before we went out on a date. He was like a commodore or something. One of those people who are on ships and wear those funny hats."

Ernie bit his lip to keep from laughing. "An admiral."

"Yeah!" Chad pointed at him. "That man was dangerous. I tried to get Vicky to run away with me. She wouldn't. She loved her mom too much. We finally split up. I remember hearing something about her dating some older guy who drove an expensive car."

Sharyn sat forward in her chair. "Yes?"

"That's about it. I didn't pay much attention after that. She was damaged goods, you know?"

Ernie wondered about that. "What made her damaged?"

Chad shrugged his absurdly broad shoulders. The movement made the padding in his suit stand out. "You know. She was with someone else after me. Not that there was any comparison. I saw him once. Plain. Old. Nice car, though."

Ernie pulled out the photo of Clint Walker. "Is this him?"

Chad looked at the photo. "Yeah. That's him. She wouldn't let him come to the school to pick her up. I followed her to where she met him at the Piggly Wiggly. It was too bad they tore that place down, wasn't it? They had the best Moon Pies."

"I always thought Moon Pies were the same everywhere." Ernie didn't bother to hide his laughter.

"Well, they kind of are. Some are fresher than others. And you can't get them in Chicago at all. They have these things called Dingalings that kind of come close." Chad seemed to realize that he was rambling and changed the subject. "I can't believe that the commodore let her date that old geezer. He would've shot him for sure! Unless, maybe, he didn't know."

Sharyn and Ernie thanked him for his time. They left his office with autographed pictures of Chad and football-shaped key rings with his company logo on them.

"I wish I would've bet you some money on that one before we went inside," Ernie said as they went back out to the parking lot. "My money is still on the admiral. I think we should get a search warrant and look for that Ruger. That might solve the whole thing."

She picked up the phone and called the DA. Eldeon Percy wasn't happy about the idea but he agreed to get the warrant for her when she told him what she knew from her interviews. "There you go. I'll let you take care of that."

"You're a sore loser, Sheriff. You can't be right all the time. And you were right about looking at Walker's murder from this direction."

"Thanks. But this information backs my theory, too, you know. Vicky could still be responsible for shooting Walker. Even if we find the Ruger at the admiral's house, that doesn't prove which one of them did it."

"I got a feeling most people aren't going to believe a fifteen-year-old girl shot a man and buried him with a bulldozer," Ernie argued. "The admiral had a strong motive, he owned the gun, and he's a believable assailant."

"You missed your calling as a lawyer," she marveled. "But you still haven't proved your case to me."

ADA Toby Fisher was waiting at the office with the search warrant for the admiral's house. "I hope you know what you're doing, Sheriff. Mr. Percy is very unhappy with this turn of events."

Sharyn took the warrant and gave it to Ernie. "I'm

not too happy about it, either. But we have to find out the truth."

He shrugged, dismissing the event, then continued flirting with Cari.

Sharyn called Nick and told him what they found out about Vicky.

"So she *was* dating Walker. The admiral should've had him put in jail instead of shooting him." Nick summed up her thoughts.

"Ernie's looking for the Ruger. He thinks if he finds it at the admiral's house that it hangs him for Walker's killing."

"But you don't think so?"

She doodled Rosemarie Marshal's name on some paper and looked at it. "Stan told us that Mrs. Marshal was overly critical of Vicky and drove her crazy. With Chad telling us that Vicky dated Walker, it probably means she lied to us. If those two women were friends in school, she knew about it, too. I think I'm going to look her up and see what I can find out about her before I throw in the towel on this."

Nick was surprised. "You think Mrs. Marshal was involved somehow?"

"I don't know. You've got all those prints from the car. Have you ID'd any of them yet?"

"We've got both Mrs. Walkers," he read from his list. "Plenty of Clint's. A slew of unidentified ones. I checked the admiral's prints on file. They don't match any we've found so far."

"Could you check Vicky's? I wonder if we could find a set of Mrs. Marshal's prints at the same time."

"I'll look," he promised. "I've got a class. Talk to you later."

Sharyn tried to get in touch with Jill. Her secretary sounded worried when she told her that she hadn't heard from her boss all week. "She's missed two court dates. That's just not like Jill. Her husband went to Raleigh to look for her. Maybe we should file a missing-person's report. I just don't know what to do."

"I'll check into it," Sharyn told her. "Do you have any idea where she was going in Raleigh?"

"I took a look at her online calendar. She was supposed to meet someone named Tom at a coffeehouse in Cameron Village. But that was three days ago. No one's heard from her since then."

Sharyn wrote down the information and promised that she'd find some answers. She put down the phone. Her heart skipped a beat when she thought about Jill laying somewhere in an alley, a victim of Jack Winter's revenge. She called a friend of hers who worked for the police in Raleigh. She gave her Jill's description along with the description and license plate of her car.

She hoped Aunt Selma wasn't right. She knew she'd never forgive herself if something happened to the lawyer. She shouldn't have agreed to their partnership. Jill didn't realize what she was letting herself in for.

ELEVEN

THE PHONE RANG AGAIN. It was Admiral Vendicott's doctor. The admiral had died from complications following his stroke about twenty minutes before. Sharyn thanked him for calling and hung up the phone. "This just keeps getting better and better." She dialed Ernie's number to let him know what happened at the hospital.

He was already in the admiral's house. "It might be just as well, Sheriff. He had more guns than Nick! And one of them is a Ruger semiautomatic pistol. A man his age shouldn't have to go through the prison system anyway. He'll just have to answer to a Higher Authority."

"Bring it in. Nick should be able to tell us if it's the right gun." At this point, she thought there was little chance that it wasn't.

Ernie didn't gloat. "I'll see you in a few minutes. I'm gonna go ahead and drop this off at the lab. I suppose it doesn't really matter now, but it'll close the case anyway."

Sharyn hung up the phone and decided to get out of the office. She was exhausted. The battleship-gray basement walls were closing in on her. "I'm going to walk down to the hospital. Nick might be able to go ahead and test the gun Ernie just found and we'll have all of this wrapped up. Call me if you need me."

Trudy frowned at her. "You look like you should go home and take a nap instead. But I'll call if I hear anything."

It wasn't as hot that afternoon. The rain had washed the heat away like Aunt Selma said it would. Low-hanging clouds rode over the tops of the Uwharries. Sharyn looked at the debris that was still left from the emergency crew cutting up the oak tree. It was hard to believe the day could be so calm and peaceful after the wild night.

Ernie pulled into the hospital parking lot as Sharyn got there. "For what it's worth, I'm sorry the admiral was involved with this too. I think he was a good guy who got put in a bad situation."

"Something doesn't fit right," she said. "Maybe it's just blaming the whole thing on a dead man who can't tell us any different. I don't know."

Nick was waiting for them and took the Ruger from Ernie. "I heard about the admiral. From what you told me, he was a man after my own heart. Maybe I'll be able to buy his gun collection."

"Yeah," Ernie agreed. "He really knew his guns. He had some fine pieces."

Sharyn's eyes narrowed as something finally clicked in her brain. "What did you say?"

Ernie shrugged. "What did I say?"

"About the admiral knowing his guns." Sharyn

turned to Nick. "We've talked about this before. Would you take this gun out to kill someone?"

He didn't have to think about it. "*No!* The Beretta should've done the job."

She paced the basement floor, lost in her thoughts. "No gun collector worth mentioning would've bothered with the .22. He would've made sure he had enough bullets for the Beretta. And the admiral told me I was lucky that he wasn't younger or he wouldn't have missed that day at his home. He said he could shoot the wings off a fly ten years ago."

Ernie scratched his head. "What's she talking about?"

"She's finding reasons why the admiral didn't kill Walker," Nick explained.

"Oh, no! Oh no, you don't!" Ernie tried to stop her. "I'm right on this one. He had motive. He had opportunity. The murder weapons belonged to him."

"Not quite," Nick reminded him. "We haven't found the heavy equipment that *really* killed Walker."

Sharyn stared at them. "There's an easy way to find out. Ernie, call your friend at the shooting range. That's pretty close to the admiral's house. I'll check online."

"I guess that puts me testing this gun to see if it's the right one." Nick gave himself a job.

She smiled at him, distracted, then went to use his computer.

An hour later, Ernie dragged himself back into Nick's office and slumped in a chair. "I talked to Jeff. The admiral was there almost every day."

Sharyn didn't look up from the monitor. "And?"

"The admiral lied to you. He could *still* hit the head on a nail from a hundred yards. He could've taken you out that day."

"I found seven awards locally for competition shooting. He won the turkey in last year's Turkey Shoot."

He stared at the ceiling. "So what does that mean? He still had motive."

"Not any more than ten other people we've talked to."

"He constantly threatened people with guns. He even tried to shoot you."

"He was a hothead." She logged off Nick's computer. "But he was too good a shot not to have killed Walker on the first try. Even if he only had one bullet for the Beretta, he would've taken him out with that."

"And if he were going to take another gun with him," Nick joined in, "he wouldn't have taken this Ruger."

Ernie glanced at him. "But it was the gun that shot Walker, right?"

"Yeah. Right gun. Wrong man. I agree with Sharyn. Even if he only had *my* collection, he would've taken something else. But being a collector, I would've gone with plenty of ammo for the Beretta. I wouldn't need two guns."

"Any prints?" Ernie asked hopefully.

"Both guns were well cared for. They were wiped, cleaned, and oiled before they were put away."

"Fine!" Ernie got to his feet. "But if the admiral didn't do it, who did?"

Sharyn felt certain now. "I still think Vicky did it."

"I can see that," Nick considered. "Except for the heavy equipment it took to move the car and bury it. Most fifteen-year-old girls wouldn't know how to operate that kind of equipment, even if they had access to it. Whoever pushed that car into the hole knew what they were doing. They didn't just ram into it."

That made her pause. "Yeah, I know. What about those prints I asked you to check out?"

He put on his glasses and looked at his folder. "Most of the prints in the car were too smudged. The few that weren't didn't match Vicky's. As far as Mrs. Marshal, I couldn't find anything on file for her. Get me some prints and I can take another look."

"I guess that means we're nowhere and we start from scratch tomorrow, right?" Ernie glanced at his watch.

"I suppose so. Go on home," she said. "I'll call you if the top of Diamond Mountain falls off."

He grinned at her. "That's the *only* way I want to hear about anything tonight."

"That's one happy man." Nick watched him leave. He sat down in the chair Ernie had vacated. "But you don't look too happy. What's up?"

Sharyn told him about Jill. "I'm really worried about her."

"I don't blame you. You should've known that you have to get at this guy with the law. We work *for* the law. Anything else is against it."

"It must be nice to wrap it up so neatly." She walked around the desk towards him. "Technically, you're right.

We're supposed to be the good guys. I try to work in the system. But with someone like Jack, the system supports him. He *was* the system here for too long."

Nick put his arms around her. "Why don't you go home and get some sleep? I don't even know what's holding you upright. I'm going to see what's keeping that information about the equipment that buried the car. I'll bring some pizza by with me later."

"Okay. Extra peppers?" She kissed him and started out of the building. Marvella almost knocked her back down the stairs as she ran up. "Where's the fire, Deputy?"

Marvella's face was excited, her brown eyes were huge. "I think I found something, Sheriff. I think I found a clue."

"What is it?" Sharyn didn't have the heart to tell her that it might not matter anymore.

"I was talking to Vicky's aunt. She's Vicky's mother's only surviving relative. She was telling me about how mad the admiral was when he found out that Vicky was dating an older man. They had a huge fight about it. He even threatened to put her out of the house if she didn't stop seeing him. His wife was still alive back then and told her all about it."

"That's pretty much what we found out today," Sharyn told her. "But you did a good job, thanks."

Marvella almost jumped up and down in her excitement. "But you don't understand, Sheriff! She wasn't the *only* one dating the older man. Her friend Rosemarie was dating him, too."

"What? How did you find that out?"

Marvella explained that Vicky's aunt told her that both girls were dating the same man. "I showed her his picture and she positively ID'd the victim. Then I went to talk to Rosemarie's mother. She knew about it, too. Neither woman knew who the man was. But both of them recognized Walker."

"Good work, Marvella." Sharyn glanced at her watch. "I think we'll go pay Mrs. Marshall another visit."

"We?" Marvella's grin broadened.

Sharyn took out her cell phone. "Cari hasn't worked much overtime lately. I'll get her to cover for you for a few hours with JP."

Marvella was too excited to stop talking. She rambled through all the details of the case as they drove out to Claraville. When she paused for breath, Sharyn told her what they'd learned about the admiral that day.

"So you think *both* of these women killed Walker?" Marvella scribbled in her notebook.

"They'd have one of the oldest motives in history," Sharyn replied. "Jealousy. It would make sense why two guns were involved and why the shots weren't lethal. Both guns belonged to the admiral, but Vicky presumably had access to both. The only piece of the puzzle that's missing would be how they managed to bury the car."

Marvella considered it. "Maybe Rosemarie didn't have guns to share, but maybe her daddy had the bulldozer or whatever did it."

"Good idea." Sharyn took out her cell phone. "Let me see if we can find out what Rosemarie's father did for a living."

ROSEMARIE WAS TAKING her trash can out to the end of the driveway when Sharyn drove up. "I'm on my way to Vicky's memorial service. Could you make it fast, Sheriff? I thought we said all there was to say about everything yesterday."

"New information has come to light," Sharyn told her. "I'll be as brief as I can. I wouldn't want you to miss your friend's service."

Rosemarie got out of the car and leaned against it. She didn't invite them inside. "I hope you don't mind if we talk out here. It's hard enough to leave the kids once. Frank hates when they cry like that."

"That's fine." Sharyn nudged her deputy with her elbow. Marvella was glaring at her like she'd killed her best friend. "Admiral Vendicott died today."

"I heard. He was a mean old man. Excuse me if I don't feel bad that he died."

Sharyn took out her notes. "According to what you told us, you and Vicky were best friends through high school."

Rosemarie nodded. "We were *still* best friends. I guess that's why she called me before she killed herself."

"And what time was that again?"

"I'm not sure. I panicked, trying to get out of the

house to go over and help her. It was probably eleven-thirty or eleven-forty-five."

"The phone record shows it was around that time," Sharyn agreed. "The only thing that surprised me is that the phone records show that she called her husband at work just before she wrote her suicide note. She didn't say anything to him about being upset or depressed. Can you explain that?"

"She always tells me everything! She always did. She didn't trust Stan the way she trusted me! How many times do I have to say it?"

"Yet, she didn't tell you that she was dating an older man?" Sharyn pursued. "Chad Stevens and Vicky's aunt knew about her seeing Clint Walker. How did you get left out of that loop?"

Rosemarie broke down, the same deep sobs that shook her slender frame that night at Vicky's house. "I knew about it. I just didn't want to tell you. The admiral was sick. He didn't need to be accused of killing that man. He's dead now. Can't you leave him alone?"

Marvella rolled her expressive eyes. "Come on, girl! Cut those crocodile tears and give the Sheriff some straight answers! You knew your friend was dating Walker because you were dating him, too! Didn't your mama think to call you and tell you I was snooping around? You need to develop your communications skills!"

"Thanks, Deputy." Sharyn stopped her. She handed Rosemarie a tissue.

"Hey!" Frank stepped out on the porch. "What's going on out here? Are you harassing my wife, Sheriff?"

"Oh, Frank!" Rosemarie ran to her husband and put her arms around him. "Make them go away! It's bad enough what happened to Vicky without them hounding me."

Sharyn stepped up to the porch. "Are you out of work, Mr. Marshal?"

"Is that against the law now, too?"

"No, sir. I was just wondering if you were here the other night when Vicky called your wife?"

"I was. I stayed here with the kids while she went to comfort that poor soul. There was nothing she could do for her. I wish it was different, Sheriff. But you can't keep after Rosie like this. She did the best she could for her. Even took her own medicine over to give Vicky that night."

"Medicine?" Sharyn looked up at Rosemarie.

"I don't think you should say anymore," Rosemarie cautioned her husband. "I think anything you have to say can be said to our lawyer, Sheriff."

Frank stared at her. "You haven't done anything wrong. Don't be scared to tell the truth."

"Was it Valium, Mr. Marshal?" Sharyn wondered. "Because Vicky was found with a little too much Valium in her system. Not enough to kill her but enough to keep her from fighting when Rosemarie went to visit her."

"I don't like your tone, Sheriff." Frank's voice was stern but worried. "I think you should leave now."

"When I leave here, I'm going to check with the pharmacy where Rosemarie gets her prescription. We'll know how many pills she had and when she got them. Within an hour, I'll have a search warrant for your house."

Rosemarie continued to hide her face in her husband's shoulder.

"What is it that you want her to do?" he demanded. "You can't just come out here and threaten us!"

"I'm not threatening you, sir," Sharyn said. "What I'd like you to do is find a sitter for your babies and the two of you come to the sheriff's office. Anything else gets messy and picked up by the press. I can spare your family, if you'll cooperate. And if you have nothing to hide, there's no reason why you can't sit and talk."

Frank nodded. "You're right. We don't have anything to hide, right Rosie? We'll come down and talk to you."

Sharyn went back out to the Jeep with Marvella. "Call Nick and find out where the admiral had his prescription filled. I'm pretty sure he said it was in Claraville. Check that drugstore and see if Rosemarie had her prescription there, too."

"Are you really gonna trust them to come in and have a talk?" Marvella asked as she dialed the morgue.

"I trust Mr. Marshal. But not his wife. It looks like she not only helped shoot Walker, she killed Vicky. We'll wait for them and follow them down."

FRANK AND ROSEMARIE were sitting in the sheriff's conference room when the answer came back from the pharmacy in Claraville. Yes, Mrs. Marshal had a prescription for Valium. It was filled the day before Vicky was killed. The prescription called for forty pills. There were only two left in the bottle. With normal usage, there should have been thirty-five.

Rosemarie denied giving Vicky too many pills the night she died. "I was trying to take one and most of them went in the toilet. I was holding the baby at the same time and just dropped them."

Sharyn sat at the wobbly table with them, wishing she had her old wood conference table again. It was hard to touch the table at all without it feeling like it was going to fall over. "Did you see your wife drop those pills?"

Rosemarie's eyes begged him but he shook his head. "No, ma'am. I didn't. But if she says that's what happened, I believe her."

"Here's what I think happened," Sharyn began. "I think, eight years ago, Vicky and you were both dating Clint Walker. Maybe you didn't realize it. Maybe it just suddenly got to be too much. Whatever the reason, you decided to kill him. You arranged to meet him at Union Cemetery. Vicky went into her father's gun collection and took out two guns so you could each shoot him. That way, neither one of you could say anything without getting in trouble."

"No!" Rosemarie cried. "I wouldn't do anything like that."

"You shot him and left him in his car then you buried it. No one found out about it and you felt pretty safe after a while. You graduated from school, got married and tried not to think about it. No one else seemed to miss Clint, either. Then last week, we found his body. Two gun shots were in it. The shooters weren't experts. They wounded him but he would've survived. If he wouldn't have been buried alive, he would've probably driven himself to the hospital and nothing would've been said about it. After all, he could've been put in jail for dating two fifteen-year-old girls."

"He wasn't buried alive!" Rosemarie jumped to her feet.

Frank buried his face in his hands. Rosemarie realized what she'd said and sat back down quietly at his side.

Sharyn looked at her notes. "I'm going to tell you your rights now, Rosemarie. You have the right to have an attorney present while we talk."

"Why bother?" Rosemarie's contrite attitude changed. "Vicky and I didn't kill that lying two-timer. We just shot him. You said so yourself. Why am I here at all? I can tell you what happened to Vicky, now that you know the truth. She killed herself because she was afraid we were going to get caught. She was always a scaredy-cat. She couldn't face everybody knowing about it."

"No matter what, you shot Mr. Walker. Even if he lived, you could've been charged with attempted murder. But because he was killed as a direct result of your actions, you can be charged with murder," Sharyn explained. "I think you might be responsible for Vicky's death, too."

"Vicky committed suicide," Rosemarie responded. "She was worried about not being able to do the job. So she took a bunch of my Valium then shot herself. I was at home with my family when it happened. Even Frank can testify to that!"

Sharyn didn't try to argue with her. What she said was true, for the moment. "You've heard your rights, Mrs. Marshal. Are you waiving your right to an attorney?"

Rosemarie sat back in her chair and folded her arms across her chest. "No, not at all. I can see you mean to convict me of something. I want a lawyer. Frank, see if you can take care of that for me?"

"Are you arresting her, Sheriff?" He shuffled to his feet.

"Yes, sir, I am. Right *now,* she's going to be charged with Clint Walker's murder. I also believe she killed her friend to keep her from talking about what happened. But I can't prove that *yet.*"

He looked at his wife, his eyes were full of tears. "I'll be back as soon as I can, Rosie. Don't tell them anything else. And don't worry about the kids. Mama can take care of them for now."

Sharyn had JP and Marvella escort Rosemarie to the lockup. Mr. Marshal left quietly without another look at his wife. The strain showed on his thin face. If he had it to do over, Sharyn was sure he'd find a way to lie for her or take the blame himself.

"How are you going to prove that she killed Vicky?" Cari asked Sharyn.

"I'm not sure. But we've solved a little more of what happened at the cemetery."

"It's hard to believe those two girls buried him alive!"

"Anything else on Rosemarie Marshal? Like what her father did for a living, or any other reference that could help us prove she was capable of using heavy equipment at that age?"

Cari looked at her notes. "No. Her father has worked at the same bank for twenty years. She didn't take shop in school. She *was* a Girl Scout for a while."

"Thanks anyway. Keep looking, huh? We need to understand how that part of it was possible or they'll eat us up in court."

Cari sat down at her desk. "I'd like to stay and tinker with Vicky's computer for a while, too, if that's okay? I might be able to find something else that will help."

"That's fine," Sharyn agreed. "Most of the time, I think *anything* is better than sleeping."

"I'm glad Ernie isn't mad at me anymore." Cari pulled on plastic gloves and took out Vicky's computer. "I didn't mean to cause trouble, Sheriff."

"I know." Sharyn picked up the phone. "I wonder if tomorrow is trash day in Claraville."

"I LOVE GOING out with you." Nick emptied another bag of trash. "It's always an adventure!"

Sharyn tried not to inhale as she sorted through a bag of diapers. "You're the medical examiner. I suppose I could've just told you about it and you'd be out here

JOYCE & JIM LAVENE

looking through this trash alone. I guess that means I'm
here helping *you*."

He flexed his hands inside the rubber gloves. "No,
that means I'm the forensics boss as far as the county is
concerned. I would've sent Megan and Keith out here.
They'd be in the van kissing and I'd be home reading the
newspaper. I guess that means I'm here helping *you*."

"Have you always been so difficult?"

He laughed. "As long as I can remember. I figured
it was what you love about me. As soon as I get a little
older, I'm going to be a curmudgeon."

She continued going through the garbage as she
laughed at him. There wasn't much in the squat green
can. She wasn't sure how likely it was that the clothes
Rosemarie was wearing when Vicky died were in there.
With only one bag left to go, she was about to admit
defeat. "I don't think they're here."

"And *why* did we think they would be?"

She explained her theory to him. "You remember
the night we found Vicky? Rosemarie was wearing a
white housecoat and slippers. There was no blood, no
GSR on her. She didn't hold a gun to a woman's head
and pull the trigger without getting messed up. If she
came home and showered then changed into the robe,
she could come back clean. But where are the dirty
clothes?"

"Maybe she's like me. Maybe they're in the bathtub."

She stopped and looked at him. "The bathtub? Don't
you have a hamper? How do you take baths?"

"First of all, men don't have hampers. At least, that's

what my father told me. A man can have a duffel bag but he can't have a hamper. And second, I don't take baths. I take showers. And since I don't put frou-frou stuff in my empty bathtub, I put my dirty clothes in there."

Sharyn finished looking through the last bag of trash. There were no bloodstained clothes in it. She stood up straight to ease the kink in her back. The light from the waning moon glinted on a small structure to the back and side of the house. "You know, it hasn't been too long since they got septic tanks out this way. Most people still have working outhouses."

Nick's gaze followed her line of vision. "No way. I've done that before and I'm not doing I again. If you think evidence is hidden in that old outhouse, I'm calling Megan and Keith. It might even stop them from kissing for a while."

Sharyn's cell phone rang. It was Cari. "I think I might have found something interesting in Vicky's computer. How are things going out there?"

"I'm heading back to the office so that the professionals can take over."

"I'll show you what I mean when you get back."

"Thanks, Cari."

"Is *she* still working, too?" Nick stripped off his gloves. "What is it with people? Everyone's awake all the time and working. I moved here to get away from all that."

Sharyn started up the Jeep. "Never mind that. Get

on the phone and call the kids. I want to know if there's anything in that old outhouse by morning."

"What's the rush? You've got Mrs. Marshal on one murder. She's not going anywhere."

"I'd just like to tie this up. Anything yet on what pushed the Mercedes into the hole?"

"No." He sniffed his clothes. "I smell like garbage. Do you have any idea how many types of heavy equipment there are in the world?"

They got back to the office just before midnight. Cari was waiting with JP and Marvella. They all stood looking over Cari's shoulders as she logged on to Vicky's computer.

"I didn't think to look for anything like this before," she told them. "I was looking for the note and when it was written. But I found a scheduler that had the computer call Rosemarie Marshal's home phone at exactly eleven-forty-five the night Vicky died."

"What does that mean?" Marvella wondered. "We knew she called her friend."

Cari explained, "It was set to do it. In other words, Vicky didn't have to be alive to call Rosemarie. Her computer was programmed to call at that time, on that night. Someone set it up around the same time as her death."

"Was there a message of some kind?" Nick asked.

"No," Cari answered. "The phone would've rung and there was probably a modem noise. Rosemarie could have set up Vicky's call for help. It works within our time frame. Rosemarie gets the call, tells her husband that it's Vicky and that she's going to commit suicide, so she has to go to her."

"But Vicky was already dead," Sharyn finished. "Rosemarie gave her the Valium, waited until she couldn't fight back, then held the gun to her head. She had plenty of time to go home, take a shower and change clothes. Good work, Cari. If we can find those clothes, we've got Rosemarie for Vicky's murder."

An emergency call took Marvella and JP out to the Stag Inn Doe for a knife fight and shots fired in the parking lot.

Marvella put on her hat and glanced at the hot-pink scarf on her desk. She looked up at Sharyn and left the scarf where it was. "When is someone gonna clean up that place anyway? We go out there at least once a week!"

Sharyn smiled at her. "Go teach them the error of their ways. But be careful."

JP nodded and smiled before he left. "We are always careful, Sheriff. Not only of ourselves, but of the others around us."

His partner put her hands on her ample hips. "Maybe you could *talk* them into being better people, JP. Let's go!"

Nick's cell phone rang. He yawned before he answered it. "I'm turning this thing off. I should be home in bed. Hello? What do you want?"

Sharyn waited for him to finish while she considered any *believable* way a teenage girl would know how to operate heavy equipment. She drew a blank. She'd watched people use the equipment but didn't know how to use it.

"That was the kids," Nick told her. "You wanted bloody clothes? How about a pair of jeans, a sweater and tennis shoes? They're bringing them in for comparison. We should know pretty soon if the blood matches Vicky Rogers."

Sharyn nodded, almost too lost in her own thoughts to appreciate the work that was done. "Good job! They make a great team."

"Yeah. I just hope they don't break up and go all moody on me. Keith was impossible for a while after he broke up with your sister." He put away his phone. "Can we go home now?"

She sat down at her desk. "Yeah, I think *you* can go home now. Like you said, Rosemarie isn't going anywhere. You can take a look at those clothes tomorrow."

He glanced at Cari and lowered his voice. "You have to get some rest, Sharyn. I'm getting worried about you."

"I'm fine. I just can't sleep tonight. I have too much on my mind. I'm going to do some paperwork and then go to see Rosemarie."

"I'll stay with you." He yawned. "I don't want you to stay here alone."

"Don't worry about it. Marvella and JP will be in and out all night. I'll be fine."

Nick finally gave up and went home. About twenty minutes later, Cari did the same. Sharyn started doing some paperwork but she couldn't concentrate. Picking up her keys and her jacket, she got in her Jeep and started towards the old Union Cemetery.

TWELVE

SHARYN SAT AT the cemetery for a long time thinking about what happened. She remembered passing the old pine tree coming back from Charlotte when she was a kid. She knew when she saw it from the car window that they were almost home.

Now there was a gaping hole where they dug out the Mercedes. No one had been out there to clean up the mess that was left behind. She didn't know if anyone ever would. It was easy to forget about the dead. They couldn't speak up for themselves. Ernie was right. It was almost as bad being a child or an elderly person.

Despite how people felt about Clint Walker, at least he had children and two women who grieved for him. No one except Eldeon Percy seemed to miss the admiral. Even worse, they'd been quick to blame him for Walker's death. She had to admit, it was still a possibility.

What if Admiral Vendicott found out that his daughter shot Walker? Wouldn't he be likely to cover it up for her? Did he know how to use heavy equipment? They might be able to look up his military records and find out.

But unless a bulldozer or another piece of machinery

was sitting alongside the road, he'd have a tough time finding one and getting it out there before anyone noticed the Mercedes in the cemetery eight years ago. The highway was a main road. The car wouldn't be able to sit out there without hundreds of people seeing it during the daylight hours.

If the admiral covered up what his daughter did, he had to do it at night, before anyone noticed that Walker was missing. There was no way for him to know that no one would bother to tell anyone that he was gone. That brought her back to how he got the machinery. He couldn't have rented it during the night. And the murder didn't look that well planned.

Without a definitive answer, Sharyn headed for home. She tried calling Jill on her cell phone. There was still no answer.

She spent time trying to decipher the codebook again. She tried using her father's favorite song, "Big John" as a key, substituting words she found from the song for other meanings. Nothing. She stared at it until the letters and numbers swam in front of her eyes, finally giving up in frustration. She was going to have to find professional help to understand the book. The logical place to look seemed to be the internet. Not even Jack had arms long enough to reach to China.

She awakened to the sound of someone pounding on her front door. When she got up, she realized that she'd slept in her uniform. Yawning, she looked at the alarm clock she forgot to set. It was almost ten! "Just a minute!"

Ernie looked at her and took charge. "Take a shower and get a clean uniform. I'll make you some coffee. Have you eaten anything?"

She smiled and rested her head against his shoulder for a moment. "What would I do without you?"

Nick's voice cut through the sounds of traffic from the street as he shut the outside door. "This is the part where I'd be really jealous except that I *know* you think of Ernie like a father. Could you start calling him dad or something, just for my sake?"

Ernie slipped his arm around Sharyn's shoulders. "You have to be *first,* old son, if you want to compete."

Sharyn shook her head. "Let's not start that. You're both very special to me."

"Yeah. But which one of us is *more* special?" Nick demanded.

"Ernie. Because he didn't ask that question. What's up?"

Nick folded his arms across his chest. "I was going to tell you two hours ago. Apparently, I was the *only* one up all night. But now, since Ernie is *more* special—"

"On second thought, don't tell me yet. I'm going to take a shower and change clothes. Ernie, will you—"

"—get you an egg biscuit to go with your coffee? Sure thing."

"I give up!" Nick threw his hands up in the air. "If anyone needs me, I'll be at my office. Not that I expect anyone to need me around here. Except when it comes to going through trash or eating really bad Thai takeout."

An hour later, showered, dressed and fed, Sharyn

stood in the hospital morgue. Nick was there with Megan and Keith. Ernie was lounging in a chair set against the side of the ugly green basement wall.

Nick gave the go-ahead to his assistants. "It's your show."

Keith cleared his throat. "Well, despite the constant interruptions, including diving into an outhouse, we were able to discover what the article of clothing is that we found at the site of the Walker murder."

"It's a vest." Megan picked up the plastic bag that held it. "We did some things to reconstruct it. It's a little technical so we won't go into that. You guys probably wouldn't understand anyway."

Nick's look was intimidating.

She smiled. "Except for you, of course, Nick. But you're not a layman."

"Well, anyway." Keith took over for his partner. "We discovered that not only is it a vest but it's a *county* vest. You know? One of those florescent orange things with the stripes that are supposed to keep people from hitting road workers? You just can't tell it right now because it's been outside for so long."

Ernie nodded. "You mean one of those 'working inmate' vests?"

"No!" Megan disagreed. "Not that kind. This one says 'Montgomery County' on the back. I don't think whoever wore it was an inmate. But whoever it was probably used the equipment that buried the car."

"Is there any reason for that conclusion, besides what it says on the back?" Sharyn asked her.

"We found a couple of things inside of it that seem to point to a private user." Keith adjusted his glasses and produced a scrap of paper with a flourish. "There were initials on an inside tag. They were written with indelible marker so we could still make them out."

Megan held up another bag. "We also found this inside the vest."

Sharyn looked at the bag. "It looks like a woman's scarf."

"Great!" Ernie said. "Marvella did it!"

"Marvella isn't the only woman who wears scarves." Sharyn looked at the piece of paper Keith used to produce a photocopy of the initials inside the vest: JS.

"That could be a *ton* of people dating back eight years," Ernie suggested. "I suppose since there's a woman's scarf in the pocket, it must be from a woman. I'll check with the county for workers with those initials."

Sharyn looked at Keith and Megan. "You've done a great job. Thanks. Are we any closer to knowing what pushed the car into the hole?"

"We are. We've matched the marks on the bumper to the pan on a CAT 977L. That's a crawler loader," Megan answered. "We figure it was a piece of county hardware since the vest was out there, too. Maybe whoever buried the car didn't realize the vest dropped out of the crawler loader. Presumably, it was dark and she was nervous."

"Of course, this could be another dead end." Ernie said. "Somebody might've parked out there while they were working on the road. They just happened to drop their vest and forgot about it when they came back for the machinery. It doesn't make them guilty of murder."

"That's true," Sharyn agreed. "We need more. What about prints?"

"There was one clear print inside that wasn't too deteriorated," Keith explained. "We're checking that out. I can tell you that it didn't belong to the admiral, Vicky Rogers, Clint Walker or either of his wives."

Ernie grimaced. "I expect I'll be checking the county records for those initials the rest of the day."

"What about the clothing that was found in the outhouse?" Sharyn asked Nick.

"Oh, so *now* you need me! Why is it always associated with bloody clothes or dead bodies?"

"Nick!"

"Okay, I'll take what I can get." He made a show of putting on his glasses and picking up his report. "The clothing found in the Marshal outhouse was splattered with Vicky Rogers's blood."

"Thank you." Sharyn smiled at him. "You did a good job, too."

"Do I get a pat on the head and a dog biscuit now?"

"No, but you can call the DA and tell him that you're filing Vicky's death as a homicide. Thanks for all your help."

"Sheriff?" Megan stopped her. "Don't ever ask us to go into an outhouse again. We've decided that we'll quit next time."

Keith looked startled. "Quit? When did we decide

that? It wasn't that bad. Everything was dry. Really. It wasn't any worse than going in that car. The smell—"

"I'm negotiating here! Remember? I'm better at this than you."

Nick stopped the discussion. "Well, negotiate *this*. You guys clean up and maybe I'll give you money for the malt shop."

"Malt shop?" Keith looked at Megan. "Now you've done it! He's going to spend an hour telling us about his childhood at the malt shop."

Sharyn took Nick aside while his two assistants argued. "That was mean."

"I know. But it was fun. And what else do you have assistants for except to torment?" He grinned. "Do you have something secret you want to tell me? Or are you just trying to make Ernie jealous now?"

She kissed him. "I don't think Ernie's jealous. He has Annie back. Thanks for working on this."

"I was up most of the night, drank two pots of coffee, and had to reuse the grounds for the second pot. Don't I deserve more than just a peck on the lips?" He slid his arms around her waist.

"Yes, you do. We'll talk about that later."

He sighed. "I can live off my imagination all day. Thanks."

She laughed and walked out into the bright sunlight with Ernie.

"Okay," Ernie started, "we've got Mrs. Marshal for her friend's murder. We know that the two girls shot Walker. But you gotta be thinking about how the DA is gonna present this case without being able to prove how the girls buried Walker in the car."

"We definitely need that," she agreed. "And maybe if you can find out who that vest belongs to, we can answer that question, too."

"If a piece of heavy equipment was available close by that night," he said, "anyone *could* have done it."

"Anyone who knew how to use it. I don't think either one of those two girls knew how. I don't think a jury will buy that ,either."

"But maybe it was the admiral covering up for his daughter." Ernie snapped his fingers. "Bet you didn't think of *that* until now."

"It's possible. He *did* have a motive. And he probably didn't realize that Walker was still alive. Let's check his military records." She went up the stairs to the courthouse beside him. "Why are you so eager to get the admiral on something with this? Usually, you're all about giving a vet a break."

"I don't know," he admitted, holding the door for her. "I think he was just a mean, ornery coot. And once in a while, I'd just like *my* hunches to be right!"

When they got to the office, Cari was frantically trying to answer the phones.

"Where's Trudy?" Sharyn looked around.

"I don't know. She was here. Now she's not. I called in a couple of volunteers to take her place. Maybe she got sick and went home." Cari picked up another phone. "How does she do this all by herself?"

Ernie laughed. "It's like learning to pick up a full

grown horse by lifting a colt every day as it's growing up. Eventually, you just don't think about it anymore."

Sharyn and Cari both stared at him.

"I'm gonna get to work on that county vest," he said, going to his card table desk. "You ladies take your time figuring out my words of wisdom."

Cari worked with him on the computer after a few volunteers came in to take Trudy's place. Sharyn went out on a call after Joe told her he needed help at an accident scene. Ed, like Trudy, had disappeared before the shift started. Joe recalled seeing his partner at the office, then couldn't find him when it was time to go. Sharyn could only speculate on what happened to the lovebirds.

When she got back to the office, Ernie and Cari had finished their search of the county records. "Find anything?"

"Not much," Ernie answered. "They weren't working on the highway at the time Walker was killed. They worked over there the year before and, again, two years later. So it was no accident the equipment was there."

"And there weren't many women working for the highway department back eight years ago. All of them were secretaries. And only one woman in the past thirty years had the initials JS." Cari put the information on her desk. "She was an accountant. I don't think she ever wore a vest. Besides, she passed away last year. She was eighty-two. I don't see her going out there and burying that car with a crawler loader."

"What about the admiral?" Sharyn asked, looking at the paperwork.

"I can't find anything in his records about operating heavy equipment," Ernie answered. "He was on a ship during his enlistment. It's unlikely."

Cari sat down at the computer again, pulling up names from the county employment file. "There *was* a county highway supervisor with the initials JS that year. But it was a man. He had access to heavy equipment. But I guess that's another dead end, huh?"

Sharyn sat very still, her hands folded on her desk. "What was his name?"

"John Schmidt." Cari looked up from the file. "He still works for the county."

All of the pieces came together in Sharyn's mind. Mary Jo's strange reaction to hearing Walker's name. Eldeon Percy telling them that Walker hit on every woman he met. It broke her heart to realize that John could be involved in this. Maybe that's why she didn't see it sooner. She didn't *want* to see it.

"No!" Ernie kicked a trash can when he saw the look on her face. "No *way!* That just didn't happen. There has to be another answer!"

Slowly, Sharyn picked up her hat and walked around the desk. "You don't have to go. I'll take care of it."

Ernie settled down at once but there were tears in his eyes. "No. You shouldn't have to do it alone. I know you hate it, too."

Cari looked at both of them but didn't ask. Whatever it was, she'd find out later.

JOYCE & JIM LAVENE

SHARYN PULLED THE JEEP in front of the Schmidts' house
in the Diamond Crescent subdivision. There was a party
going on. Red, white and blue decorations were everywhere.

"That's right," Ernie observed. "Johnny was coming
home today. He's back on leave from the Middle East for
two weeks. John and Mary Jo were so excited about it."

Sharyn squinted through the sunshine at the old
crawler loader that was sitting on a trailer beside the
garage. It still had its county marking even though John
had bought it at auction years ago. She'd already called
Megan and Keith to check the markings they had from
the bumper of the car against the pan on the loader. But
instinct told her they'd match.

She remembered when John used the piece of equipment to dig out the patio at her parents' house. He and
Mary Jo stayed for a barbeque after they were done.
She and Johnny played in her pool together. Fighting off
those memories and hardening her resolve, she walked
up to the house, praying that, somehow, she was wrong.

Michael, Johnny's brother, met her at the door with
one of the twins in his arms. He grinned at her. "You're
just in time, Sharyn. Johnny got here a few minutes
ago. Come on in."

The family was noisy and happy to see their return-
ing relative. Uncles, cousins, gathered in the house.
Sharyn and Ernie knew most of them. They were wel-
comed like family and offered something to eat.

"I need to see John," she told Michael after not finding his father in the sunroom. "Is he around?"

"Yeah, we carted him out to the backyard." Michael's smile faded as he saw the grim look on her face. "Is something wrong?"

She couldn't tell him. She couldn't find the words. "I need to talk to him."

Michael knew something was wrong. He walked through the house with them. He handed the baby to his wife as he passed her, but didn't answer when she asked what was wrong. The three of them filtered through the crowd until they reached the backyard.

John was sitting under a newly budding, weeping peach tree. The white-and-pink blossoms perfumed the air and littered the ground. The Schmidts were starting work on a swimming pool when John was injured. There was a partial hole dug, covered with a tarp.

"Sharyn! Ernie!" John greeted them. "I was hoping you'd show up today. Where's Ed?'

Sharyn sat in a lawn chair beside him. She took off her hat. "John, we have to talk."

He nodded. "Okay. What's the problem? Is it Caison and your mother again? Because I—"

"It's about Clint Walker." She lowered her voice. "We found your vest. It was buried next to the car."

He leaned his head back against his chair. "I was wondering what happened to it. Hoping I lost it somewhere else, I guess. All these years."

"It had your initials inside. And Mary Jo's scarf, I think." She paused and looked around then explained his legal rights. "Would you like to tell me what happened?"

His expression hardened as he gripped the arms on

the chair. "That man shouldn't have been born. You've checked up on him. Was there anyone who mourned him? Even his own kin didn't report him missing. The world is a better place without him. I'm not ashamed of what I did. He was like a rabid dog in heat. And I know you've figured out that I wasn't the only one involved. I heard the news."

Ernie closed his eyes and lowered his head as the other man spoke.

"I thought he was dead that night. I found him in his car, slumped over the steering wheel. I thought…" John's voice choked on the words. "I thought Mary Jo killed him. I knew she'd been slipping out and seeing him on the side. They met at a VFW picnic. I didn't realize anything at first. Then she was gone too much, too often. I followed her and saw them together. He had other women. Why did he need her?"

Sharyn put her head in her hands as she listened. It was almost more than she could bear. John was a good man. How could this happen to him?

His voice was tense as he continued. "He and Mary Jo quarreled. He'd been out with a hairdresser or something. When I found him in his car, I just wanted to save Mary Jo. I took her scarf out of the car and put it in my pocket so they wouldn't find it. Then I thought about her fingerprints being in there. I had the crawler loader on the trailer behind the truck. I decided to bury him in the car."

The laughter of the children running around the yard and the smell of hamburgers on the grill made a surreal backdrop for his confession. Sharyn heard Ernie move uncomfortably beside her. No doubt the same strange sense of what was happening affected him, too. He'd known the Schmidts even longer than she had.

"I swear I didn't know he was still alive," John said with a sob in his voice. "I wouldn't have done it if I'd known. I hated him but I wouldn't have killed him. I was only trying to protect Mary Jo."

Michael was waiting just out of earshot. When he saw his father break down, he rushed over to him. "That's enough! What's wrong, Sharyn? What's going on? Why are you torturing him?"

The partygoers began to realize that something was happening. They spilled out of the house and shushed the children. The hamburgers burned, unattended, on the grill. Johnny started towards them in his dress uniform.

Before Sharyn could answer Michael's questions, there were cries of alarm from the family room. Mary Jo emerged from the sliding-glass doors with a gun in her hand. She ran through the crowd. People screamed and scattered around her. Her face was mottled by tears as she focused on John.

"We've got a problem." Ernie got to his feet and put out his hands as she approached them. "You don't want to do this, Mary Jo. Don't make it worse. Give me the gun."

"I know what happened." She sobbed. The gun shook in her hand as she pointed it first at Ernie, then at Sharyn. "I didn't realize until I heard you asking about

Clint. Then I saw the look on John's face and I *knew*. He only did it for me. Because I was stupid enough to fall under that man's spell. John doesn't deserve to go to prison. I won't let you take him."

Ernie kept moving towards her. "Mary Jo, somebody's gonna get hurt. You've got all the little ones over here today. I know you don't want them to see you this way. Please give me the gun."

"Mama, do as he says. Please!" Michael pleaded with her.

"*No!* Ernie, you and Sharyn leave him alone!" Mary Jo waved the gun back and forth again. "John can't go to prison because of me. He's a good man."

Sharyn didn't move. Mary Jo was too distraught. She was capable of shooting at least one of them before they could get her down. Ernie was too close. He could grab the gun but it would probably go off.

"Mary Jo, sweetheart," John whispered hoarsely into the sudden quiet in the yard. "Put down the gun. Don't do this to yourself. We've had a lot of good years together. We both made a mistake. You've been paying for yours for eight years. Now I'm going to have to pay for mine."

"Don't say that, John. We can fight this together. No one has to know."

"It's too late for that, honey. Can't you see that?"

"No!" Mary Jo screamed and pointed the gun at Sharyn.

Ernie moved quickly and grabbed the weapon. It went off as they fell to the new green grass together.

Sharyn and Johnny ran towards them as people started screaming.

"Get the kids inside!" Michael yelled at his wife.

"Ernie?" Sharyn separated him from Mary Jo. There was a spreading red stain on the left side of his uniform.

Johnny cradled his mother in his arms. "She's fine. I think she fainted." He raised his voice. "Somebody call an ambulance."

Ernie opened his eyes as Sharyn unbuttoned his uniform and looked at the wound. "Nick won't like this at all."

"Just keep still. You were lucky. The shot hit your shoulder. You'll probably get some time off, though. That's what you were going for, wasn't it?"

"Yeah." His teeth were chattering from shock. "That was it."

She squeezed his hand. "You know, when I said I'd shoot you so Annie would feel sorry for you, I was only kidding. Besides, you two are already back together."

He closed his eyes. "You can't always have all the fun."

The ambulance arrived a few minutes later. The paramedics stabilized Ernie and assured Sharyn that the wound wasn't life-threatening. They asked a few questions about how it happened. Michael and Johnny were huddled around their parents with the rest of the family inside the house.

Ernie grabbed Sharyn's hand and whispered, "Not Mary Jo, too."

She nodded. He didn't have to explain any further.

Somehow, she'd find a way to keep Mary Jo's name out of her report. What was going to happen to the family was tragic enough. She didn't want to be responsible for Mary Jo going to jail, as well.

Johnny stayed with his mother as she regained consciousness and started to cry. Michael waited until the paramedics took Ernie then he approached Sharyn. "What will happen now?"

"I have to take your father into custody. I'll have an ambulance transport him to the infirmary at the county jail."

"Isn't there something you can do?" Anger darkened his face. "Our families have been like kin. Can't you help him?"

She wished she could. She wished there was some way to change all of it. But that wasn't possible. "I'm sorry. I'm the sheriff. I have to do my job. Your father killed a man. He has to be responsible for his actions."

"And what are we supposed to do without him? I believe you'd find a way if it was *your* father."

Sharyn picked her hat up from the ground. "The first thing you need to do is be grateful that Ernie isn't going to have your mother put in jail, too. Do you realize what the penalty is for holding a gun on a sheriff's deputy, much less shooting one? The next thing you need to do is get your father a good lawyer. Maybe a jury will have some leniency on him. That's the best I can tell you."

Everyone watched as Sharyn did her job. She arrested John Schmidt for the eight-year-old murder of Clint Walker then she read him his rights. The ambulance arrived to take him to the county jail. She told the guard that John didn't need to be handcuffed in front of his family.

"Thank you, Sharyn." John shook her hand. "You're a good sheriff and a good friend. I'm sorry you had to go through this. I know it wasn't easy for you. I'll have a talk with Michael. He'll understand. Tell Ed we'll have to make that game another time."

John was the *only* one in his family who felt grateful for her being there. She could feel their angry stares as she walked through the house. Where there had been laughter and conversation before, there was only silence and weeping as the truth of what happened set in. She got on her cell phone and called Eldeon Percy to let him know about the arrest. The DA was glad the admiral's good name was cleared but he was saddened by John's guilt.

Sharyn drove to the Diamond Springs' Presbyterian Church and sat on the little stone bench by her father's grave for a long time. It was a terrible arrest. One she would never forget. Not that she could forget any of them. But Michael was right. These people were like family to her. She'd done her job, but her heart wasn't in it. If she could've looked the other way, she would have.

No one said being the sheriff would be easy. It came with plenty of price tags. Her privacy. Her freedom. Sometimes, like today, her soul. "But you know that, don't you?" she asked of her father and her grandfather where they slept in the good earth beside her.

The wind whispered down from the mountains and

rustled through the new green leaves on the oak tree above her. The air smelled like spring; full of life and promise. Sharyn said goodbye to Jacob and T Raymond and drove back to the office.

SELMA'S MEMORIAL DAY parties were legendary in Diamond Springs. Everyone from town showed up to cluster around the beehives and taste the fresh honey. The azaleas were in high bloom along with the wisteria and the honeysuckle. It never rained during the party. The sun was always shining for those few golden hours.

Everything was red, white and blue, including the food and Aunt Selma's dress. Streamers floated in the breeze and the smell of fresh baked bread perfumed the air.

Sharyn walked with Nick through the crowd and sampled the food. Everyone congratulated her on solving another murder case. "I wish I *felt* successful."

"Quit knocking yourself around about it," Nick answered. "He was your friend but he helped kill a man. You did what you had to do."

"I know. I guess I wish people weren't so happy about it."

Selma handed her a glass of blackberry wine. "Guaranteed to be good for what ails you. Don't you deserve a vacation or something?'

"Nick and I are going hiking in the mountains," Sharyn told her. "No cell phones. No radios. No problems."

Nick nudged her. "Look! The prodigal couple returns!" He pointed to Ed and Trudy as they walked across the grass towards them.

Trudy grinned and held out her left hand. "We ran down to South Carolina and got married! Can you imagine? We eloped!"

The men shook Ed's hand and the women looked at Trudy's ring. The sunlight glinted on the diamond on Trudy's slender hand.

"I hope you're both looking for new jobs," Sharyn teased. "You could've called in before you left."

"We knew you'd understand, Sharyn." Trudy hugged her. "I'm sorry for what you went through with John and Mary Jo. But be happy for me!"

"I am." Sharyn returned her hug. "I just hope you know what you're getting into."

Trudy wiped tears from her eyes. "You never *really* do, you know. But you have to take the chance. You know what I mean?"

Sharyn glanced up at Nick over the crowd that suddenly separated them. He saluted her with his glass of wine. "I'm afraid I do, Trudy. They can be a handful. But I guess they're worth it."

EPILOGUE

SHARYN FINALLY FOUND a cryptographer who was interested in the black book. He was a student at the University of Indiana. They'd emailed back and forth a few times. She didn't tell him who she was or where she was. It was hard to believe that Jack could find out about what she was doing, but she didn't want to take any chances.

She scanned in a few pages from the book and sent it to him. She was reading his email, telling her he'd received the pages and would get back to her as soon as he could. He warned her that it could be a lengthy process and asked her to be patient. Despite her impatience to know what was in the book, she knew she had no choice. She wasn't able to decode it. All she could hope was that he could understand it.

The phone rang and she glanced at the clock with a groan. It was just past four in the morning. If there was an emergency—and she'd spent her whole night online—she was going to pay for it in the morning. "Hello?"

"Sheriff Howard? This is Mary Stanton, Raleigh PD. You asked me to keep an eye out for your friend, Jill Farmer?"

"Yes." Sharyn's attention left the monitor. "Have you found her?"

"Yes, ma'am. We've got her in lockup right now. Caught her downtown selling crack, high as the proverbial kite. She'll be arraigned in a few hours."

Sharyn frowned. "Is that Jill *Madison*-Farmer? From Diamond Springs?"

"That's what her ID says, yes, ma'am."

"Okay. Thanks." Sharyn was already shutting down her computer and looking for her car keys. "I'll be there."

* * * * *

REQUEST YOUR FREE BOOKS!

2 FREE NOVELS
PLUS 2 FREE GIFTS!

Your Partner in Crime

WWLI3R

REQUEST YOUR FREE BOOKS!
2 FREE NOVELS PLUS 2 FREE GIFTS!

HARLEQUIN

INTRIGUE

BREATHTAKING ROMANTIC SUSPENSE

YES! Please send me 2 FREE Harlequin Intrigue® novels and my 2 FREE gifts (gifts are worth about $10). After receiving them, if I don't wish to receive any more books, I can return the shipping statement marked "cancel." If I don't cancel, I will receive 6 brand-new novels every month and be billed just $4.74 per book in the U.S. or $5.24 per book in Canada. That's a savings of at least 14% off the cover price! It's quite a bargain! Shipping and handling is just 50¢ per book in the U.S. and 75¢ per book in Canada.* I understand that accepting the 2 free books and gifts places me under no obligation to buy anything. I can always return a shipment and cancel at any time. Even if I never buy another book, the two free books and gifts are mine to keep forever.

182/382 HDN F43C

Name _____ (PLEASE PRINT) _____

Address _____ Apt. # _____

City _____ State/Prov. _____ Zip/Postal Code _____

Signature (if under 18, a parent or guardian must sign)

Mail to the **Harlequin® Reader Service:**
IN U.S.A.: P.O. Box 1867, Buffalo, NY 14240-1867
IN CANADA: P.O. Box 609, Fort Erie, Ontario L2A 5X3

Are you a subscriber to Harlequin Intrigue books and want to receive the larger-print edition?
Call 1-800-873-8635 or visit www.ReaderService.com.

* Terms and prices subject to change without notice. Prices do not include applicable taxes. Sales tax applicable in N.Y. Canadian residents will be charged applicable taxes. Offer not valid in Quebec. This offer is limited to one order per household. Not valid for current subscribers to Harlequin Intrigue books. All orders subject to credit approval. Credit or debit balances in a customer's account(s) may be offset by any other outstanding balance owed by or to the customer. Please allow 4 to 6 weeks for delivery. Offer available while quantities last.

Your Privacy—The Harlequin® Reader Service is committed to protecting your privacy. Our Privacy Policy is available online at www.ReaderService.com or upon request from the Harlequin Reader Service.

We make a portion of our mailing list available to reputable third parties that offer products we believe may interest you. If you prefer that we not exchange your name with third parties, or if you wish to clarify or modify your communication preferences, please visit us at www.ReaderService.com/consumerschoice or write to us at Harlequin Reader Service Preference Service, P.O. Box 9062, Buffalo, NY 14269. Include your complete name and address.

HIDIR13R

ReaderService.com

Manage your account online!

- Review your order history
- Manage your payments
- Update your address

*We've designed
the Harlequin® Reader Service
website just for you.*

Enjoy all the features!

- Reader excerpts from any series
- Respond to mailings and
  special monthly offers
- Discover new series available to you
- Browse the Bonus Bucks catalog
- Share your feedback

Visit us at:
ReaderService.com